Blade is under more pressure than ever. Mary is
dying, Jaz is still missing, and the spectre of Becky is
haunting him once again. Danger stalks him wherever
he goes and, to make matters worse, his greatest
enemy from the past is now back in his life.

But all is not lost. Blade has his courage, his will, his
sharp intelligence—and he has a hostage, someone
who will give him real bargaining power. Blade is not
finished yet, not by a long way. His blood is up and
he's ready to mix it.

The sixth title in this ground-breaking series from
Tim Bowler, the Carnegie Medal-winning author
of *River Boy*, *Starseeker*, *Frozen Fire* and *Bloodchild*.
Blade knows exactly what he wants—and he'll
stop at nothing to get it . . .

BLADE
MIXING IT

Other Books by Tim Bowler

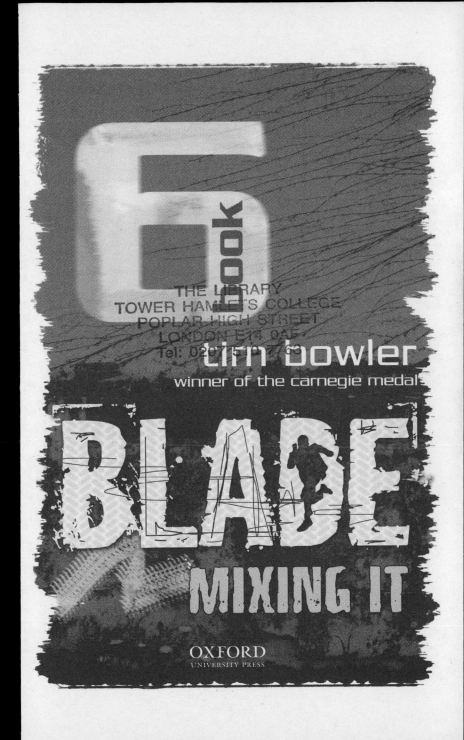

OXFORD
UNIVERSITY PRESS

Great Clarendon Street, Oxford OX2 6DP

Oxford University Press is a department of the University of Oxford.
It furthers the University's objective of excellence in research, scholarship,
and education by publishing worldwide in

Oxford   New York

Auckland   Cape Town   Dar es Salaam   Hong Kong   Karachi
Kuala Lumpur   Madrid   Melbourne   Mexico City   Nairobi
New Delhi   Shanghai   Taipei   Toronto

With offices in

Argentina   Austria   Brazil   Chile   Czech Republic   France   Greece
Guatemala   Hungary   Italy   Japan   Poland   Portugal   Singapore
South Korea   Switzerland   Thailand   Turkey   Ukraine   Vietnam

Oxford is a registered trade mark of Oxford University Press
in the UK and in certain other countries

British Library Cataloguing in Publication Data

Data available

ISBN: 978-0-19-275399-5

1 3 5 7 9 10 8 6 4 2

Printed in Great Britain by CPI Cox and Wyman, Reading, Berkshire

Paper used in the production of this book is a natural,
recyclable product made from wood grown in sustainable forests.
The manufacturing process conforms to the environmental
regulations of the country of origin.

For Rachel
with my love

Not a word from Lord H at the other end of the phone. And I know why. The bastard's waiting for me to speak. He knows I will. He knows I've got to. Cos he knows he's stronger than me.

I might have kidnapped his son, might have little Damien trembling next to me on the front seat of the car, freaking his head at the sight of my knives. But it makes no difference.

The silence goes on. Like a scream.

Cos Lord H is stronger than me.

Lord H.

Yeah, yeah.

I picture his face. He won't have changed at all. He'll be fifty-two now but he'll still look like he's forty. Younger even. An aristo god, master of all he surveys. Blue eyes, sculptured cheeks, hair the colour of a kiss.

If it wasn't for the mouth, you'd say it was a kind face. And he can make it look kind when he wants to, even with the mouth. He can make it look anything. Only I know better. Cos I know the face too well.

Haven't seen it for three years, but I remember it good enough. The picture I usually get is me sprawled on my front and him peering down at me from on top. He's got a hand under my chin and my head yanked up so he can mock me in the eyes while he has his fun with me.

He liked that. Mocking, humiliating. There was nothing I could do to stop him. Cos the truth is, Bigeyes, he was just too strong. All I could do was keep telling myself no one could hurt me if I belonged to him.

But that was before Becky died.

And the whole world went quiet.

Like this phone in my hand. A small, quiet thing, its silence seeping into me. I can feel that power again, and it's not coming from me. It's coming from Lord H, like it's always done.

I got to fight it.

Somehow.

Glance at Damien. Kid's curled up on the passenger seat, eyes flicking over the knives on my lap. I speak into the phone.

'You know what I want.'

Still silence.

'And you know who I got here.'

I take a long, slow breath.

'You took Jaz. Or your goofs did. And I want her back. So give her up and you get Damien. Simple as that. But listen.'

I take another breath. Got to keep my voice calm. Got to sound like I'm in control. Even if I'm not.

'You get what you give, OK? If Jaz is dead, then Damien's dead too.' I stare down at the knives. 'And so are the rest of your kids.'

Damien starts sobbing again.

Yeah, I know. I hate doing this, Bigeyes, but I got no choice. There's too much at stake now. So I got to play it rough.

I can't mess with this slime. He wants his boy back but he's cold as steel and twice as hard. And that's not the worst. The worst is he's clever. Cleverer than anyone you'll ever meet. And more ruthless.

Don't be deceived like everybody else.

'Here's how it's going to work,' I say.

Still the silence. It's deeper than ever now. I can feel his hatred churning inside it, cold and dark. I force myself to go on.

'You get your goofs to drive Jaz to the police station. The one in New Cross Road. They stop outside, leave her by the main entrance, drive off. Someone'll be waiting for her.'

I pick up one of the knives.

'When I hear she's safe, I'll ring you again. And tell you where you can find Damien.'

Wait, listen.

He's never going to buy this. He's going to want a straight swap, both kids together. That way he's got a chance of slamming me too. He'll never hand over Jaz and take my word I'll ring him about Damien afterwards.

'You got an hour,' I mutter. 'An hour from now.' I check the car clock. 'If she's not at the station by ten, I'll take it she's dead. And you know what that means for Damien.'

I squeeze the knife tight.

'And in case you're wondering, cos some of your slugs might just have told you I've lost my bottle, there's something you got to know. I'm not going to kill Damien myself. I'm going to hand him over to less pleasant people.'

I pause.

'Like Nelson or Fitz or Jimmy-Joe Spice. Or one of the others. There's plenty of bojos who'd like a piece of your kid. If you think I'm bluffing, try me.'

Damien starts wailing nearby.

Still silence down the phone. Freaking me bad now, Bigeyes. Cos I can't work out what he's thinking. I could once. Or I thought I could. But not any more. Then it happens.

The click at the other end of the line.

And he's gone.

Lean back in the driver's seat. I'm shivering. Trying not to but I can't stop. Got to do something, get a grip. Can't let Damien see me scared. Check him out. He hasn't noticed what I'm like. He's still wailing and he's turned away again, his face pressed against the side window of the car.

I stare past him at the garage wall beyond.

This isn't going to work, Bigeyes.

Lord Slime's never going to do what I want. And maybe he can't anyway. If Jaz is already dead, what can he do? On the other hand, what if Jaz is alive? There's still just a chance. And I got to act like there is.

Cos there's not much else I can do.

'Damien,' I say.

He doesn't answer, doesn't turn. Just keeps on crying, face against the window. I don't blame him. Jaz must have been the same. Blasted out of her head. But I don't want to think about that.

'Damien, I'm not going to kill you.'

Or hand him over, Bigeyes. Before you ask. I never intended to give him up to Nelson or the other gangsters. But I can't tell him that now. I just want him to stop crying. First cos I got to make another call and I don't want the sound spilling down the phone. And second . . .

Cos I just want him to.

He curls up tight, hands clasped over the back of his head. But the crying eases off, turns into a sniffle. I can handle that. Look down at the mobile, punch in the number. Funny how it comes back. Like all the other numbers. Don't ask me how I do it, cos I don't know. I just remember stuff.

Press Dial.

Ring, ring.

He better bloody answer. It's not a whack like it was with Lord H. Slimeface was always going to pick up the phone. But this one's different. Still, I got a couple of backup numbers if the call doesn't work.

Ring, ring.

Come on.

Ring ring. Answerphone kicks in. Grumpy voice. Hasn't changed.

'Inspector Bannerman—'

'Yeah, yeah.'

'I'm not at my desk right now—'

'Lazy bastard.'

'But if you leave your name and contact details after the beep—'

I hang up, key in another number.

Ring, ring. This one's his mobile. Let's hope he's—

Shit. Voicemail.

'Bannerman speaking. Can't take your call right now but if you—'

Hang up, glance at Damien, back at the phone. Last number I got. Key it in.

Ring, ring.

'Hello?'

Woman's voice. Wasn't expecting that. Maybe he's moved. Cos I mean, there was no way he was ever going to get a wife. Not with a face like that. But maybe he's got a sister.

'Who is this?' she says.

I know that voice, Bigeyes. I've heard it before.

'Haven't got all day,' she says.

I make myself speak.

'Is Inspector Bannerman there?'

'*Inspector* Bannerman?' she says.

'Yeah.'

'Is this a police matter?'

'Might be.'

'Because if it is,' she goes on, 'you should be ringing the police station, not here. This is a private number.'

And suddenly I get it, Bigeyes. The voice. And I can't believe it. I can picture her face, clear as his, clear as my own in the car mirror. But it's not her face I remember most about her. It's something else. Something big.

Bosoms.

That's what I remember.

And that's what I called her. When I was seven. What the hell's she doing answering his private phone? It can't be what I'm thinking. No way. Not with him.

'Ring the station,' she snaps.

'It's Jonny Bell,' I say.

Intake of breath at the other end. I can feel her thinking. She was about to hang up. She still is. Don't ask me how I know. Sound of a door somewhere near her, footsteps coming close. Someone muttering, Bosoms whispering back, then a new voice in my ear. A new, old voice.

'Jonny Bell,' it says.

'Inspector Bannerman.'

He gives a sneery chuckle.

'Or are we Billy Nail today? Or Richie Finch? Or Jimmy Stoko? Or Frankie Reeve or Stevie Black or—'

'Going through the whole list, are you?'

'Don't suppose I know the whole list,' says Bannerman. 'And even if I did, there's not much point reading it off. Life's too short for your fantasies. So let's keep it simple. Why don't I just call you Blade?'

'Yeah, why don't you?'

I give a sneery chuckle of my own.

'Pugface.'

Bannerman snorts.

'Pugface? That your name for me? I think you can do better than that.'

'I got others.'

'I bet you have.' He sniffs. 'So how did you get my home number?'

'I've always had it.'

'You never used it before.'

'Don't tell me you're disappointed.'

Bannerman grunts.

'So what's this about? Giving yourself up?'

'No.'

'You should. It's pointless running.'

'You got to help someone.'

'Who?'

'A three-year-old girl. She's called Jaz. She's—'

'I know who she is,' says Bannerman. 'And I know about Rebecca Jakes. And Trixi Kenton. And her brother Dig. And all the others. Including the elderly Irish woman.'

I feel myself stiffen.

'Mary,' I murmur.

'Yes.'

I swallow hard.

'Is she . . . I mean . . . is she still alive?'

'I don't have any information about her.'

'Cos last time I saw her, she was really ill. She was—'

'I don't have any information about her.'

Silence. I don't know what I feel. Just know it hurts. Like thinking about Becky hurts. Bannerman goes on.

'How can I help the little girl?'

His voice sounds sharp, like he wants me to hurry on. And I'm glad. Cos I want to hurry on too. Can't be thinking about Mary. Not right now. There's no time to waste.

'You got to move quick,' I tell him. 'You and what's her name?'

'Who?'

I can't say Bosoms, Bigeyes. Even to Bannerman.

'Who?' he says.

'The woman who answered the phone.'

'DI Fern?'

'Yeah. You got to ring the station. Right now. Tell 'em Jaz is going to be dropped outside the main entrance some time before ten.'

'How do you know?'

'Never mind. I don't know what state she'll be in but it's going to be bad. They're not to mess with the people leaving her there. Probably won't get a chance. They'll drive off quick. But someone's got to be there to look after Jaz.'

Bannerman doesn't answer but I hear him muttering to Fern. Can't catch the words but I hear her say, 'OK.' Nothing for a bit, then I catch Fern's voice talking on another phone. And here's Bannerman back.

'Now then,' he begins.

But I cut him short.

'You got to get there too, Bannerman. You and Fern.'

'There'll be people waiting at the station.'

'I want you there. And Fern.'

'We can't get there right away.'

'You got to be there. Both of you. For when Jaz turns up.'

'What for?'

Because she's got to meet the right nebs, Bigeyes. It can't just be anyone waiting for her. I'm not mad on porkers at the best of times, but I got time for Bannerman. And if Fern's his squeeze or his mate or whatever, that's even better. Cos she's decent too.

They'll help Jaz.

And that's all I care about.

'Never mind why,' I mutter. 'Get to the station and I'll ring you later.'

'Why don't you just come in?'

'Why don't you just shut your mouth?'

I hang up, lean back again. Shivering like before. Not so bad as with Lord H, but I'm choked, Bigeyes. Head's full of stuff I can't handle. And now they're back again. Bloody tears. They're swilling round my eyes and I can't stop 'em.

And worse.

I'm moaning, shaking, slamming my head with my fists. Damien's peering round, his own eyes drenched up, his mouth gaping as he stares at me. I stare back, try to get a grip.

But I can't. The tears keep flooding, then something bursts out of me, a kind of bellow. Can't hold it back. I feel my hands clutch the knives, squeeze. I close my eyes and howl into the dark.

Feels like ages before I stop. When I do, I realize I've curled into a ball just like Damien did before. I can feel it, even with my eyes still closed. I've got my knees pulled into my chest, my hands clasped round the ankles. Must have let go the knives cos they're tucked into my lap, and the top of my head's pressed against the steering wheel. I can feel it chafing against the wound in my brow.

I keep my eyes closed a bit longer. Don't want to open 'em. Not yet. I take a long breath. Feels juddery, like my lungs don't want to work. Take another breath. Just as hard. Open my eyes, look round.

Damien's not there.

I stiffen. Passenger door's open, no sign of the kid. I feel a flutter of panic, grab the knives, scramble out of the car—and there's the boy. Far corner of the garage, slumped against the wall.

Never heard him get out. I must have been in a bad state to miss that. He could have got away maybe, if he'd had the spit. But he's still too scared. He looks up, watches me standing by the car, shrinks closer to the wall.

I call over.

'I'm not angry with you.'

He doesn't answer. Just goes on watching, his face dark.

And I'm wondering, Bigeyes. Does he see my darkness too? He must. He's seen me break down, heard me moan and howl and sob. He can't be scared of me still, can he?

But he is. Look at him.

Choked out of his wits.

Maybe he thinks I'm even more dangerous now I've cracked in front of him. And maybe he's right. Maybe I am more dangerous. Truth is, Bigeyes, I don't know what I am any more. Or what I can do.

I used to know. Used to be bung-clear about all that.

And it gave me confidence.

Now I got none.

'I'm not angry with you,' I say again.

Don't know why I'm repeating myself. He just looks more scared every time I open my mouth. I look down. Still holding the knives, see? Same old problem. Like my hands are magnets. I grabbed the bastards without thinking.

Look back at Damien. Still watching me.

With those dark little eyes.

I drop the knives on the seat, close the door, edge round the front of the car towards the boy. He starts to whimper, press himself back against the wall. I stop moving, call out.

'Easy, kid.'

He goes on whimpering.

'Easy, kid.' I sit down on the bonnet, look down at him. 'I'm not going to hurt you.'

He keeps his eyes on my face.

I stare at him. Hard to think this boy's got such a father. If only he knew what his dad's really like. But he won't have a sniff of that. How could he? How could anyone? Cos you know what?

Only a handful of nebs know what Lord H really is. His wife and children certainly won't. Nor will his relatives, or his friends. Or the nebs who run his charities. They only see the caring family man, the great public benefactor.

And one of the richest guys on the planet. He was already that when he was born. Only it wasn't enough, Bigeyes. He's a business supergun too and he must have earned his inheritance twenty times over.

But let's give the bastard his name. And Nanny keyed it pretty good in her mobile—Lord H. Which kind of hits the spot. Only there's something about the H Nanny won't realize.

It hits the spot twice.

First there's the name she knows. The official name.

Lord Haffler-Devereaux.

Yeah, I agree. Fancy prick of a name. But don't worry. We don't need to use that. Not you and me, Bigeyes. Cos he's got another name. Another H name. And Nanny won't know that one. Practically nobody will, not even his wife, or his kids, or the thousands who work for him, or the government nebs who listen to his advice.

It's a name only the other slimeheads know. The ones at the top of his organization. The handful, the chosen few. The puppet-masters who are slowly cutting the cords that hold this world together. The ones behind the charade.

I told you about it before.

The Game.

They all got names, these players. Secret names for their secret lives. Want to hear 'em? Then listen. And remember.

Raven, Swan, Swift, Owl, Condor.

And then our man—Lord H. Worked out the H? Course you have.

Hawk.

That's what the other slimeheads call him.

And it fits pretty good. Cos you know what? For all his looks, charm, and manners, that's what he is. He roams like a hawk, sees like a hawk, kills like a hawk. And you never know he's there till it's too late.

I feel Damien's eyes on me. Stare back at 'em. Is that Hawk looking out at me? A future Hawk? Who's to know? Can't see one now. All I can see is a scared kid. He wipes his eyes and drops his head.

I reach into my pocket, feel for one of the mobiles, pull it out. It's the one I creamed off that ancient gobbo in the car park. Dimpy old phone. But who cares? Long as it works.

Too early to ring the police station. Jaz can't possibly be there yet. If she's going to turn up at all. But I can't help it, Bigeyes. I got to try Bannerman again. It's just possible.

Punch in the number. I'm trying his mobile first. He won't have hit the station yet but someone might have rung him already with some news.

Ring, ring.

This is stupid. It's much too early to phone. I got to be patient.

Click.

'Bannerman speaking.'

'It's Blade.'

'What do you want?'

'Any news of Jaz?'

'Give us a chance. We've only just left the house.'

I can hear the sound of the car. And Fern talking in the background. Jesus, Bigeyes. What's she saying? Who's she talking to? Can't catch the words. It better be someone from the station. It better be good news.

'Ring me later,' says Bannerman. 'I'm driving. Or better still, come in to the station.'

'Piss off.'

'Suit yourself.'

Sound of a car horn, a growl from Bannerman. Fern still mumbling in the background.

'I'm hanging up,' says Bannerman. 'Ring me later.'

'Wait!' Fern's voice nearby. 'Hold on!'

More muttering, one to the other, then Fern's voice in the earpiece.

'Are you there?' she says.

'Yeah.'

I stare back at Damien. He's watching me close

again. And suddenly I see it, just for a moment, in those small, six-year-old eyes. The hawk, peering back.

Marking prey.

Though he doesn't know it yet.

Fern speaks again. And there's a shiver in her voice.

'They've got Jaz.'

I feel the words rush out of me.

'Is she alive? Is she alive?'

'She's . . . alive,' says Fern.

She hesitated, Bigeyes. Did you hear that? She definitely hesitated. And she spoke quiet. Something's wrong. I slam in quick.

'What's happened?'

'I just told you,' says Fern. 'She's alive.'

'You hesitated!'

'Don't shout down the phone.'

'I'm not shouting!'

But I am, Bigeyes. I can't help it. I got to know what Fern's holding back.

'Tell me!' I bellow. 'What have they done to her?'

Silence at the other end. I see Damien staring up at me, mouth open. Fern answers, same quiet voice.

'I don't know what state she's in. I haven't got any details. We're still on our way to the station. I just know she's alive.'

'But you hesitated!'

'I hesitated because of you.'

I clench my fists, try to understand. But it won't come. I'm so fizzed about Jaz, about wanting to know she's OK, I can't think straight. Fern speaks again.

'I hesitated because of you.'

'What about me?'

'You surprised me.'

'Eh?'

Bannerman takes over the phone.

'You surprised her. And me.'

'I wasn't talking to you, Bannerman.'

'You were shouting so loud down the phone you were talking to both of us.'

I don't answer.

'And we were both surprised,' he goes on.

'What about?'

'You caring for the girl.'

'What's wrong with that?'

'Nothing. We just didn't think you were capable of it.'

'Capable of what?'

'Caring.'

His words stab me. I catch Damien still watching, look away towards the side wall. Can't bear the sight of his eyes, not when I'm trying to get my head round this other stuff.

Not capable of caring.

Not capable.

So what about Becky? Eh? What about Mary? I care for them. Not bloody capable. I feel the tears start again. Cos the trouble is, Bigeyes—Bannerman's right. Deep down I know it. I didn't use to care. Not till I met Becky. And when she died, I stopped again. Till now. But Bannerman won't know that. Nor will Fern. Or anyone else.

Why should they?

He speaks again, hard voice.

'Come into the station. Come now. It's the right thing. And we'll let you see Jaz.'

'Yeah, right,' I mutter. 'Before you take her away.'

'Do you expect us to keep her for you?'

I don't answer.

'Eh?' he says. 'You must have known this was going to happen when you fixed for her to get dropped at the station. And you did fix that, didn't you? It's not an accident. Or something you just happened to know about. You fixed it, didn't you?'

I still don't answer. But he's right about Jaz. Course he is. I always knew what was going to happen. Thing is, Bigeyes, what else could I do? Jaz can't live with Bex. And she certainly can't live with me. Or the troll-gang from the old city. Bex won't be pleased but she'll have to deal with it.

And so will I.

But I still can't bear the thought of never seeing her again.

'She's not yours,' says Bannerman. 'Are you listening? You're not her father or her brother or her guardian.'

'Piss off.'

'She doesn't belong to you. And she doesn't belong to Rebecca Jakes. If you've helped get her to the police station, that's good. It's a mark in your favour. But that's all. She's not yours to keep. It's for other people to take over now. There's a system in place to help kids like her.'

'Yeah, sure. Like the system that helped me.'

There's a pause. Think he's handed the phone back to Fern. Yeah, he has. Here's her voice again.

'Are you there?'

I don't answer.

'Come in to the station,' she says. 'You can't stay on the run for ever. Give yourself up.'

She's talking gentle, like she's coaxing. Makes me think of Mary. Mary told me to give myself up too. And I was going to, remember? Had it sorted in my head. Before the grinks took Jaz. And killed Dig.

Maybe that's what's waiting for me, Bigeyes.

A knife through the heart. Like he got.

Glance back at Damien. And for another small moment, I see that look in his face. Yeah, yeah, he's still what he was—a frightened kid. Yet somewhere in those scared little eyes I can see the hunter that'll come looking for me one day.

If his dad doesn't get me first.

'I'm not giving myself up,' I mutter.

And hang up.

Silence again. Feels so deep I'm scared it's going to swallow me. I listen for sounds outside. There they are—cars, smellies, stuff. The hum of the Beast as the world wakes from another misty sleep.

I look at Damien.

Still watching me.

Still scared.

If only he knew how scared I am of him.

I walk over to him, look down. His eyes widen, his mouth gapes. I want to speak to him. Say I'm sorry. But I can't. I turn away, edge back to the driver's door, reach in.

Pull out the knives.

Feel Damien stiffen again.

I straighten up, call out.

'Sorry.'

He's crying again, quietly now, not sobbing or whimpering like he was before. Just soft little tears, running down his face. I turn away, listen cute, ease up the garage door.

Light dribbles in, grizzly and grey. Spit of breeze

brushes over me. Check round. No nebs to be seen but I can feel plenty near. Got to wig it while I got a chance. Find somewhere safe. Where I can think.

But first things first.

Check inside the garage again. Damien's still slumped on the floor. He's staring out at me round the side of the motor. I call back to him.

'Stay where you are, OK?'

He doesn't answer.

'Stay where you are till they come and get you. Don't walk off on your own. And don't open the garage door.'

What the hell am I doing worrying about this kid? I shouldn't give two bells about him. But I can't be dealing with that now. Swing down the garage door, check round again.

Down to the lane, stop, glance round it.

All clear.

I know what I want to do, Bigeyes. Blast out, run my feet off. But it's no good. There's something else I got to do first. Dimpy and risky, but I can't stop myself. Check down the lane.

Remember what I told you about those buildings?

They're offices. Crumbly, useless offices. I used to bust in there sometimes when I had to slap it for a night or two.

Well, I'm busting in again. Only not for the night.

Down the lane, checking cute. Got to be dead careful cos I haven't been here for three years. I don't know what's in these places any more. They haven't been tarted up. Anyone can see that. But I haven't grubbed out the inside.

So keep your eyes open.

First gate, check round. Nobody in the lane, nobody on the other side. I reckon this building's deserted. Going to risk it anyway. Over the railing, into the courtyard, round the back to the door.

Just like it used to be.

Tatty and tired.

Listen cute.

Not a sound inside. Creep past the windows, check through. Empty rooms. Check over my shoulder. Lost the hammer when I jacked Nanny's car but this brick'll do.

Pick it up, wait, listen. Smash!

Glass breaks easy. No sound of an alarm. Flick the

catch, inch up the window, squeeze through, listen again. Still silence. Just the traffic noise beyond the lane.

And my heart pounding in my chest.

Through the downstairs rooms, soft, slow, listening cute. Not a sound inside the building, just my steps padding on the dry wooden boards. No furniture in any of the rooms, but there's paint pots, brushes and cloths at the bottom of the stairs. Someone's got plans for this place, that's clear.

Let's just hope they don't turn up for a bit.

Least this won't take long.

Up the stairs, slow, soft, checking round. First floor. More paint pots, brushes in jars, cloths and buckets, overalls. Packet of cigs, open, half-full.

Stop, listen.

Still silence.

Up the next flight of stairs. It's coming back to me, Bigeyes. Must have been eight or nine when I last came in here. But I still recognize the place, even without the desks and filing cabinets.

Second floor. Wallpaper peeling all round. Down to the landing. There used to be one last flight of stairs. There you go, behind that door. Little stairway to the top of the building.

And that's what I want.

You'll soon see why.

Up the stairs, into the little room, over to the window, kneel down. Got to keep low. No curtain to hide round and it's easy to be seen from down below. But it's a good view the other way too. Check it out, Bigeyes.

What do you see below?

The garages.

Perfect place to look down. Just got to make sure I keep myself well hidden. Let's go. Pull out the phone. I'm using Nanny's mobile again.

Scroll down.

Lord H.

Dial.

He won't speak at all this time, Bigeyes. I'm telling you. He won't even say 'Yes?' Which is fine by me.

Click.

He answers first ring. And there it is.

Silence.

'Listen good,' I say. 'Cos I'm not saying it twice.'

I tell him where the boy is, stop, wait. Don't know why. I told you, Bigeyes, he's not going to speak. I don't even want him to. I just . . . I don't know . . . want him to feel I'm not scared. Like I'm cute with the silence.

Except I'm not.

It's freaking me already.

Like before.

I hang up, drop the mobile on the floor, stamp it to bits. Slump on the boards, wait. It won't take long. They'll be here in minutes. And so will he. That's right, Bigeyes. He'll come personally. I know it.

He'll be here in ten.

He's here in five. There's a sound of motors, big, powerful beasts. I straighten up, edge to the window, slow, careful. Got to play it cute. I'm pretty sure they won't be looking for me up here. They'll think I've blasted out, fast as I can, far as I can.

Even so.

Got to be careful.

Straighten up, slow, slow. I'm keeping to the side

of the window this time, not peeping from underneath. Check down. Four motors parked outside the garages.

One of 'em's his.

Gobbos spilling out of the cars. Six, seven, eight, nine. Big dronks, shiny suits, groomed. Upper-class grinks, not the sluggy low-life that first caught up with me. But what else do you expect? The Hawk's never going to look cheap.

Why hasn't he got out?

I'm fixing his motor. You bet I am. Check it out, Bigeyes. Even the car's an aristo. It's purring with the engine off. Two figures still in it. Driver in the front, Hawk in the back. Or just the shadow of him.

Cos he's sitting far side, behind the passenger seat, head turned away. Get out, you slime. I want to see you again. I want to stick your evil face. Not cos I need to. But cos I want to.

Cos you're my enemy.

The biggest one I ever had. Or ever will.

And that's saying something, considering how many I got.

But he's still sitting there. Lets his grinks buzz over to the garage, yank up the door, bomb inside. Out again, one of 'em holding the kid. And now here's Daddy. Door of the car's opened, and he's out in the open.

At last.

Arms wide, takes the boy, hugs him close, face buried in Damien's neck, other side of the kid's face, so I still can't see what I want. All I got is the boy's cheek. He's crying. I can see from here. Crying his head off.

Gobbos edge round close. Hawk waves 'em off, mutters something. One of 'em trigs back into the garage, starts up Nanny's car, backs it out. The others spread out, check round the garages, over by the wall, back towards the lane.

Towards me.

I inch to the side of the window.

Jesus, don't tell me they're grubbing out this place. I never thought they would. Glance round the window, just a peep. They've stopped at the lane. Think they're just checking round, making sure all's cute for the Hawk. Not looking for me special.

Yeah, I'm right.

They're heading back to the motors. Getting in, doors closing, engines revving up. Only the Hawk's still standing there, Damien pressed close. Boy's still crying, Daddy stroking the back of his head. And now he's bending down, handing the boy in to one of the gobbos in the car.

And then he straightens up. Looks over.

At me.

Only he can't see me. No way. Not from there. I'm peeping round so I can clap him but there's just a shiver of me outside the window-frame. No way he can see me. No bloody way.

But I can see him.

I can see him good, Bigeyes.

Check out the face. Go on. Do it. Hair, cheeks, mouth, eyes. You can see all of 'em from here, even the eyes. OK, maybe not the eyes. Maybe I'm just remembering the eyes. But I can see the rest. And so can you.

Remember what I said? How young he looks? Ten years, twenty years younger than he is. Not that I give two bells. It doesn't matter how old he is. All that matters is how dangerous he is.

And how few nebs know that.

Or will ever believe it.

That's the problem, Bigeyes.

Cos you're looking at Mr Good. Mr Squeaky Clean. Philanthropist, Patron of the Arts, Public Benefactor, Collector and Connoisseur of Beautiful Things.

Remember that face, Bigeyes. Keep it in your head. Let it burn into you. Like it's burned into me. I hoped I'd never see it again. But I guess I was a dimp. I was always going to. And anyway, why bother about hope?

When hope's never bothered about me.

He's still looking up. Just standing there, gazing. He can't know. He can't. If he'd seen me, he'd never just stand there. He'd have his dronks snapped round the building by now, blocking the exits, crashing in. I'd be dung by now.

If he knew.

He can't have seen me.

He can't have guessed.

But he's still standing there, looking up. And I'm staring back, hidden—surely. Just the smallest part of me in his sight line, too small, too far, just the edge of one eye for him to see. He can't clap that from there.

But he still hasn't moved.

Cars nosing round him. Check that out, Bigeyes.

He's just standing there, making no room. And the big motors are creeping round him. That's power. He doesn't move for anyone. Never has done, never will. They can hardly get past without brushing him or knocking him, one side or the other.

And still he won't move for 'em.

Glances round at the nearest car. I miss the look. Can't see it with his head flicked away. But I clap the face of the driver. Yeah, mate. You're sweating, right? Cos the boss just shot one at you with his eyes.

And I know what it said.

Mess my suit and you're mince.

Car slinks past him. Others follow, crab round into the lane, stop, wait. Hawk takes no notice of 'em. Turns his head, back to me, walks forward, closer, closer, stops again, just under my window. I edge to the side, right out of view.

He can't see me now, definitely. But I can't see him either. And I don't like that. Wait, pressed against the wall, heart thumping, blood racing. Listen. Listen good. Going to be one of two sounds. Engines or a smash of glass. If it's the first, I'm cute. If it's the second, I'm finished.

Smash of glass.

I stiffen, reach for the knives, squeeze 'em tight.

Then another sound.

Engines.

And a car door slamming shut. Just one. It better be his. Jesus, Bigeyes, it better be his. Revving up, squeal of tyres, and they're pulling away. I tighten my grip on the knives, ease out so I can see through the window. Got to risk it. Got to make sure it's not a trick.

But they're going.

All the motors. And Hawk's going with 'em. I can see the back of his head as the car slips away. He's got his arm round Damien and he's cuddling the boy close. The kid looks back, just once, and I stiffen again.

But then he twists round again, tucks his head into Daddy's shoulder.

And they're gone.

I breathe out, slow, hard. Heart's still pumping. Got to check round. Make sure it's still safe. This could be a trap. He might just have clapped me up here and let a couple of his grinks sneak round to hide and pick me up on the way out.

And somebody definitely smashed a window.

Down the stairs, soft, cute. Check round, every space, every shadow. All quiet in the building. Not even a creak of the boards. Check each floor, down to the next, down to the bottom, stop.

Check again.

Listen.

Nobody. Creep round the downstairs rooms, check out the windows into the lane. Clear so far. Front room—broken glass all over the floor. Old nobbly brick lying there. He must have flobbed it in, Bigeyes.

The Hawk.

I reckon he just did. Cos he's raging. Cos he wants my blood.

And he never knew I was here.

Lucky me.

Slip the knives away, bend down, pick up the brick. Squeeze it tight. Turn and fling it against the far wall. It thunders back at me, bounces on the floor, lies still. I stare down at it.

Cos suddenly I know, Bigeyes. Suddenly it's clear. This is where we find out—who's the hunter, who's the prey. I'm raging too. I want blood too. I'm not leaving. I know that now. Not wigging it out of the Beast.

First cos I got to check Jaz is cute. Check she's looked after good. Even if I can't see her again, I got to make sure she's OK. And second cos there's things about the past I want to put right.

Right as I can anyway.

And there's something else too. Something big.

I got my enemy. Got him fixed in my head. He was there before, course he was, but now I've seen him again, he's clearer than ever. And I know this for certain.

I can't run any more. You know why? Cos he'll never rest till he's found me. Till I'm dust trickling through his hands. So I got one choice left. Bring him down.

That's right, Bigeyes.

I got to mix it.

I pull out the old gobbo's mobile, stab in the number, wait.

'Yeah?' says Ruby.

'It's me.'

She gives a grunt.

'How you get this number?'

'I remembered it.'

'I never give it you.'

'Becky did.'

'That don't make it right.'

'Can I speak to Bex?' I say.

'No.'

'Why not?'

'She gone.'

'Gone?'

'You heard me.'

'Where?'

'How do I know?'

Click of the phone as she hangs up. Silence again. Just my thoughts cracking my head. And the drone of traffic beyond the lane. I try the number again. Rings and rings, then she picks it up.

'Don't got nothing to say to you.'

'Ruby—'

'Piss off.'

'Meet me in the alley behind The Turk's Head.'

'I don't hang about in alleys. Not no more.'

'It's about Becky.'

She doesn't answer.

'It's about Becky,' I say.

I see that face again. That beautiful black face. Like I'm staring at the photo in Ruby's shrine. And somehow the real face is smiling back. Like it always did.

Except at the end.

I try to take a breath. Won't come. Feels like the air's fighting me, like it thinks I don't deserve it. Maybe I don't. I try again, gulp in a bit.

'Ruby, listen. I want to tell you what happened to her.'

'Tell me now,' she snaps. 'We don't need no alleyway.'

'I want to show you where it happened. And . . . I want to explain.'

She's quiet again. Still raging. She wants me dead so much. And I don't blame her.

'I didn't kill Becky,' I tell her. 'I promise I didn't. But . . . '

I hesitate.

'But what?' she growls.

'It's my fault she died.'

Ruby starts to sniffle.

'Ruby, listen—'

'Leave me alone.'

'Meet me behind The Turk's Head.'

'You bastard!'

I squeeze the phone tight.

'Ruby,' I mutter, 'I know you hate me, but . . . '

It's no good, Bigeyes. The words won't come. I can feel 'em freezing in my mouth. I want to put things right, I swear I do, but talking's no good now. It's too late for that. Becky's dead and nothing'll bring her back.

Ruby speaks suddenly, grit-hard.

'I'll meet you.'

'OK. Midnight.'

'No,' she slams. 'Not midnight. Now!'

'It's got to be midnight. I can't get there before.'

Yeah, I know. I'm lying, Bigeyes. I can get there before. But there's a reason why it's got to be midnight. First cos I got other stuff to do. And second— well, never mind. It's just got to be midnight, OK?

'Alley behind The Turk's Head,' I say. 'Midnight.'

Ruby hangs up without a word.

Out of the door, round the building, back to the lane. Got to blast out of this place now, wig it fast. Hawk's gone but his grinks'll be close, and they might just lick over this patch first.

Makes sense. Last place they know I was, so they'll probably sling a net round it and squeeze just in case. I've smacked it here long enough. Over the gate, into the lane. Check right and left.

Two motors parked down the far end where it meets the main street. They don't look like trouble but that means nothing. Check the other way. Garages look clear and I can always cut back the way I want to go.

Come on, Bigeyes.

Over the lane, down to the garages. Stop, flick a glance round. Looks cute. End of the row, last garage, stop again, check round. Scraggy grass down to the far wall, nobody in sight.

Round the garage, over the scrub, stop at the wall, listen. Traffic drumming past on the other side. Bit of a risk now, me suddenly appearing on top of the wall. Some driver might chuck a glint. I might even cop a grink ripping past at just the wrong moment.

But I got to go for it.

Scramble up. Brick's kind of crumbly but it's got plenty of holds and it should do. Up to the top, peer over. Taxis, bikes, motors, smellies. Wait for a gap, scramble over, jump down the other side, turn my face to the wall. Drone of engines goes on behind me. Pull up the hood, saunter down the road, face low. Catch the front of a bonnet in the corner of my eye.

Just appeared, moving slow, like it's tracking me.

Keep my face down, turned away, but not right to the wall. Got to keep half a glance on the motor. It's still there, keeping pace with me. I slow right down. It still won't cut off, just eases down, like it's stuck to me.

I stop.

It does the same.

I turn, fix it. Big motor, flash, four gobbos in it, all suits. Passenger window rolls down, guy leans out, shouts over.

'Know where Duke Street is?'

'First right, third left.'

'Cheers, kid.'

And they're gone.

Walk on, slow, hood still up, checking cute. I'm going the same way as those gobbos, only further. Whip a glance back over the traffic. Might risk a smelly if it looks safe. Or a taxi.

Got to watch good though. The grinks'll be buzzing their eyes over everything and they're going to be even more snicky now I've roughed Hawk's kid.

Over the road, first right, past the engineering works, check round. Couple of taxis. Both taken. Three more. Same again. Walk on. Smelly rumbling the other way. Trig past the parade of shops, cross over.

Another smelly. Coming up behind. Number 34.

This'll do. Long as it's safe. Run down to the stop, huddle round to the back of the queue, keep low. Peer out at the bus. Packed full. Got nebs standing down the middle. Don't like the look of 'em, Bigeyes. Might be wrong but I'm not risking it.

Doors open. Passengers pile off, my lot pile on.

Stay back, watch.

Still don't like the look of 'em.

Walk on down the street. Just didn't feel right. Didn't clap anybody. But you can't always tell grinks. I'm speeding up. Can't help myself. I feel edgy. This is bad, Bigeyes. I'm just feeling more and more scared. It's the Beast making me choke.

I keep thinking of the old city. She was tough and she could scare me too.

But she wasn't like the Beast. She had some kindness in her. Places I could go and feel safe. Not here. Every street's going to be like this. Even when there's no grink in sight. Sound of footsteps behind me. Running.

Following.

I jump over to the wall, twist round, hood still up.

Two dronks racing towards me. Black kids. Sixteen, seventeen. Dreads, glitter. No question they got blades. I brace myself, reach for the knives, hold 'em ready, under my coat. The dronks bomb close.

And run past.

Didn't fix me once.

Neither of 'em.

Smelly drums past a moment later. Still packed with nebs. And somehow they look different now.

Older. Like they're pensioners. Dunnies, half of 'em, naffing like they're on an outing. A little jaunt. Off to the zoo maybe. Or one of the sights.

One happy little smelly.

Disappears like the two black dronks.

What's happening to me, Bigeyes?

I'm jumping at everything.

Walk. Got to keep walking, keep moving. Stuff to do, whether I'm freaked or not. Shift your stump. Move, move, move.

Down the street, hugging the wall. Hands tight round the knives under my coat. Try to ease the fingers free. They don't want to let go. They want to cling on. They won't let go.

Jesus, Bigeyes. I don't know what's right any more.

I feel scared with the knives and just as scared without 'em.

Still clutching the hilts.

'Let go.'

I'm muttering aloud. Hear that, Bigeyes? That's how bad I'm getting.

'Let go.'

'Stop talking to yourself.'

And now I'm muttering back. Both ways. Speaking and answering. Jesus, I'm clapping myself over.

'Stop talking to yourself.'

'Shut up!'

Still doing it. Still bloody doing it.

Take a breath, walk on, take another breath, walk on. Step, breathe, step, breathe. And I'm still holding the effing blades.

'Let go of 'em!'

Shouting now. Blasting out the words. Or they're blasting out of me. Can't stop 'em.

'Let go! Let go!'

Gobbo on the far pavement bobs a glance. I fix him heavy. He turns away, hurries on, doesn't look back. Walk on, walk on. I'm like a dead weight. This is so bad, Bigeyes. I got no chance mixing it with the Hawk if I'm nicked in the head.

Got to get a grip. Make myself calm down. Stop, wait, take another breath. Let go of the knives. Let go of the bloody knives.

Done it.

Thank Christ.

Pull my hands out, flick the fingers loose.
Check round.
And here's another smelly.

Number 37.

Not as good as the 34. Should have hooked that one when I had the chance. But never mind. 37'll trim up the journey a bit. Long as it's safe. And long as I can get to the stop quick. Run down the street. Panting now, bung-tired. Might not make it.

Glance back. Smelly's caught behind a van. That's cute. I needed a break. Run on, reach the stop, and here's the bus rumbling in. Step back, hood flopped over my face.

Eyeshine over the passengers. Not so many nebs on this one and they look like muffins. I'm going for it anyway. Doors open, nobody gets off. Jump on. Surly gobbo behind the wheel. Snag the ticket, find a seat, face low. Doors close. Smelly rolls off.

Check round again, slow, careful. Nobody looks dangerous. They just look tired. Like I must look tired. Wonder what else they see. More than just a tired kid?

A scared kid? A terrified kid?

Maybe they don't see anything. Maybe they're not even looking. Can't see any of 'em checking me out. Maybe that's how it is now, Bigeyes. I'm just nobody. Nobody worth bothering about. The only nebs who want me want me dead.

The rest of the world doesn't give two bells.

Smelly judders on down the road. Left at the end, judder, judder, on to the next stop, pull over. Like my life, Bigeyes. Judder, stop, judder, stop. Doors open. Feel my eyes whip round. Force of habit. They just do that. Don't have to think about it. Little queue of nebs crashing on.

Muffins.

Pretty sure.

Dip my head, let the hood fall lower. Nice and dark. Only it doesn't feel nice. Doesn't feel anything. It's just dark. Hear the doors close, then it's judder again, judder bloody judder.

I meant what I said, Bigeyes. I'm nothing now. Just a creature hiding in the dark, carried from one place to the next.

'Can you move up, please?'

Woman's voice. Sounds like an old dunny. Speaks again.

'You're half over the other seat and I can't sit down.'

I snick a glance up at her. Yeah, I was right. It is a dunny. Ancient too. Got hair sprouting round her mouth. Looks gross. I check her eyes, look for some snap. But they're soft, kind, bit like Mary's. She motions to the place next to me.

'I want to sit down and you're blocking the seat.'

I grunt, give her room.

'Thank you,' she says.

Sits down, settles herself. I dip my head, let the hood close over my face again. Hope she's not going to talk. Smelly rattles off. Dunny's quiet, just sitting there. But something's wrong. I can feel her body moving. It's up against mine. And it's trembling. Don't know why.

Then I feel it.

Again.

My hands on the knives. I got 'em stuffed under my coat and I'm gripping both hilts. Tight like before. Jesus, Bigeyes. When did I do that? Eh? I don't remember reaching under my coat. Don't remember taking 'em. And why? It's an old dunny, for Christ's sake. Who's she going to hurt?

She's still trembling. I can feel her old body shivering against me. I twist my head, sneak a look. Catch her staring at me, eyes wide. Maybe she's ill, got some medical condition. No, it's not that. Not with those eyes. She's choked out. And it's cos of me. I know it.

'Don't hurt me,' she murmurs.

She looks down at my coat, checks round like she's trying to attract attention. But nobody's watching. Looks quickly back at me.

'Don't hurt me.' She's pleading, low voice. 'I know you've got something under your coat. A knife probably. I can't see what it is but I felt you reach for it. You're still holding it. I can tell. I'll give you my purse. Just don't hurt me.'

'I'm not going to hurt you.' I stare at her. 'And I don't want your money.'

She doesn't believe me. Look at her face, Bigeyes. Bungs another glance round. Still nothing from the other passengers. Nobody's noticed yet but they will soon. They'll clap she's not right. And they'll fix me straight. I got to stop her before she calls for help.

'I haven't got a knife, OK?'

I let go of the blades, pull my hands out, show 'em. 'See?'

She stares at 'em, looks up at my face. Still not sure.

I shrug.

'And I don't want your money.'

I give a huff, turn away, stare out the window. Just praying she keeps quiet. I don't need trouble from a dunny. Feel her stand up, edge away. Glance round. She's heading for the back of the smelly. Finds a seat, sits down, sees me watching, looks away.

I do the same.

Feel a shudder of pain.

Drop my head, pull the hood right over. Tears start again. I grit my jaw, breathe hard. Bastard tears. Got to stop 'em. I screw my eyes up, scowl into the dark. Hold 'em in somehow. But I'm wailing inside. Like Jaz that time I freaked her in the old hulk. When my face scared her so bad. And now I've freaked an old dunny. And I didn't mean to.

Can't take any more of this. Stand up, hood still low, walk to the door of the bus, hold on to the rail.

Not looking back at the dunny. Not looking at anyone. But I can feel her watching. And the other nebs. All my instincts tell me they're watching.

All the nebs on the bus.

Maybe I'm wrong. My instincts aren't what they were. Don't know why. I've lost something. Since Mary and Jaz. Since Becky even. Far back as then. Since the day I found I couldn't kill any more.

Maybe no one's watching.

Not even the dunny.

And I'm just freaking my head for nothing. Cos I've lost it, Bigeyes, lost everything. I'm staring at the bonnet of the bus. Pull over, you bastard. I got to blast out of here. But the stop's another quarter of a mile.

I can still feel the wailing. It's deep inside me, like someone's screaming to get out of me. And I know who it is, Bigeyes. It's me. Screaming to get out of who I am. But I can't. I'm locked inside myself, like I'm locked inside this effing bus.

Change in the sound of the engine. Driver's crunching down the gears. Slowing down, bus stop pulling close. Nobody waiting. I glance round, check the faces. Looking down or away. None of 'em watching me. Not even the dunny.

She's talking to an old gobbo in the next seat.

Feel the smelly come to a halt.

Doors open. I stumble off, down the street, not looking back. Hear the doors close, engine rev. Moment later the smelly rolls past. I turn my head away. Don't want to see the dunny watching me. Wait till the bus has grumbled round the next bend, fix the street again.

Lots of nebs trigging up and down. Muffins, far as I can tell. Taxis, motors, bikes, more smellies. Cut down the next street, right at the end, through the playground, down the alley, out into New Cross Road.

And now we got to watch, Bigeyes.

Not just for grinks but for porkers. Cos this is where Hawk's dregs dropped off Jaz. Big building over there. See it? Halfway down on the right. And there's something they'll know. All of 'em. Porkers and grinks.

They'll know I won't keep away.

Cos of Jaz.

They'll know I'll be drawn to this place.

Like I am.

Don't suppose I'll get a glimpse of her. But I can't help myself. She's in there somewhere, Bigeyes. That big dronky building. They won't have taken her out yet. I'm sure of it. She'll be sitting in there. With Bannerman and Fern, I hope, or some decent porker.

I just hope she's OK.

I can't bear to think about what's happened to her.

I got pictures in my head, Bigeyes. I know the rooms in that place. Been in there myself enough times, specially up to the age of seven. That business I told you about with Bannerman and Fern, remember? The pedestrian crossing when I was seven?

In that building. That's where I was. And I've been in lots of the other rooms.

So where is she? My beautiful Jaz.

Down the street, keep behind the parked cars. Edge closer to the entrance. Check it out, Bigeyes. Steps up to the door. That's where they'll have dropped her. Bottom of those steps. Then crashed off in their motor.

She'll have stood right there. On that spot. Or maybe sat there.

Was she crying? Do you reckon she was crying? What state was she in? And here's another thing, Bigeyes. I didn't tell you this before, but I'm worrying about something else. What if Fern was zipping me over? She said Jaz is alive. But how do I know she was telling the truth?

It might have been a trick.

To get me to come in. Thinking I'd get to see Jaz. When she was never even there. That's what haunts me, Bigeyes. The thought that she might even be dead. Spite of what Fern said.

Nebs coming out the door. Pull back, crouch, check over the road, cute as I can. Two porkers in uniform, gobbo and a woman. Don't know 'em. Third neb. And I recognize her straight up. But it's not Jaz.

It's Bex.

She's got her head bowed and she's sloping down the steps. Looks choked out of her brain. I'm watching good, checking hard. Woman's got a hand hooked round Bex's arm, but not clamped. Looks almost motherly.

Making no difference.

Bex is freaked.

And I'm suddenly remembering something, Bigeyes. Think back, right? First time I rubbed shadows with her and we had a proper talk. After we wigged it out of the bungalow. She said something about the porkers, remember?

About being scared of 'em.

Not wanting to meet 'em, cos they'd send her back.

That's the word she used.

Back.

Only where's back? I'm starting to guess, Bigeyes. And it's cos of something else she said, another time, something about her dad. What he used to do to her on his boat. Are you cracking this? Eh? Cos I am. I'm seeing it clear. I got no proof and I could be wrong.

But I'm not.

OK?

I'm not.

Cos there's a third thing I remembered. Just now. Bex's name. All of it, I mean. Funny how I never thought about it before. Never clicked it in my head. But it's banging away now, like a mad screaming voice. That name, that bloody name.

Rebecca Jakes.

Jakes, Jakes, Jakes.

There's a porker called Jakes. Big dronk, high up in the police force. And he lives in the Beast. Another district, not close to here. I used to do jobs round his patch. Never brushed his stump. Kept clear of the bastard.

And he was a bastard. All the bums said so.

If he's Bex's dad, no wonder she looks bad.

Police motor drawing up. They're getting in. Gobbo bends down, opens the door, nods Bex in the back. Courteous, old-fashioned even. Woman's climbing in after her. Gobbo lumbers round the other side, climbs in too. Three in the back, Bex in the middle.

Yeah, yeah.

The porkers are being nice.

And careful too.

She might be freaked, but they're watching her

cute. And now I'm getting the other thing. Clear as the pounding of my heart. The porkers didn't find her. She just gave herself up. Don't ask me how I know. And she's given up more than just herself.

She's given everything up.

Hope, caring, the whole stack.

I can guess what happened. She walked out of Ruby's place and up to the nearest porker. Or came straight to the station. Said here I am. I'm done. Finished. Jaz is gone and I've had enough. I got nowhere to go, nothing to care for. I know what's waiting for me.

The law.

And my dad.

But I don't care.

Car passes and she's gone. Christ, I feel bad. But I got to move on. Got to push Bex out of my head, got to act as if Jaz is really alive, and move on.

Back down the road, left at the end, left again, down to the crossroads, over to the park, through it and out the other side, down the steps to the bus stop. Wait, hood over my face. Smelly rolls in. Number 14.

Check the passengers, jump on, ticket from the driver.

Smelly rumbles off.

Two stops, three, four, checking faces. They're like bubbles in the sea. Floating on, floating off, too many to count. But I count 'em. I check 'em all.

Fifth stop, sixth stop.

Seventh, eighth, ninth.

Off the bus, left past the café, through the alley-way, out into the estate. Stop, under the walkway. Check round.

Check again.

Block of flats. Dronky brickwork, peeling window-frames. Kids kicking a football against the garage door further down. Gobbo bellows at 'em from inside the bottom-floor flat. They kick the ball one more time and wig it, laughing.

Silence.

I reach inside my coat, feel for the knives.

Slip round the building, in the back entrance, up to the first floor, wait. Still quiet. Up to the next floor, and the next, and the next. Not taking the lift. Too risky. Too easy to get boxed in.

One floor to go.

Still no sounds. It's like this place belongs to ghosts. Top floor. Down towards the end. Flat 22. Same colour door. Same stain on the outside. Same lock even. He might have moved. But I don't think so. Too lazy to shift his stump.

Ear to the door, listen. Usually got the television on when he's in. Or the radio. Or both. Even if he's got a woman. Which he usually has. Don't ask me what they all think. But they got to stack it or wig it. Cos the dungpot won't live without noise.

What did I tell you? Hear that?

Television on. Some game show. And another sound. Fainter, but you can clap it if you listen good. Hear it? Don't tell me I got to explain what it is. Try the door, soft.

Locked.

Down to Flat 23.

Stop, listen. No sound from inside. Listen again. Ring the bell, step back into the shadow, wait, watching both doors. Nothing. Just the sound of the television from Flat 22. And the other sound.

Back to Flat 23, whip out the knives. Lock picks

easy. Open the door, snick in, close it behind me. Listen, feel, watch. No one here. I'm sure of it. But I got to check. Kitchen, loo, bedroom, lounge.

Dronky place.

Nobody here.

Pick up a chair, carry it over to the balcony door, step out. No sign of anyone watching from below. Take a breath, lift the chair, ease it over the rail onto next door's balcony, climb after it.

Squeeze the knives. One in each hand.

Peer through the door into Flat 22.

Nobody in the lounge. Just beer cans on the sofa and clothes on the floor outside the bedroom. Pick up the chair, stand back, fling it at the balcony door.

Glass shatters like a scream.

From inside the flat comes a bellow, but I'm already through. I'm into the lounge and racing for the bedroom. Door opens and there's his face peering out. Startled, scared, but still dangerous. Twenty-one years old and he's muscled out since I last saw him.

'Jesus!' he mutters.

Sees the blades coming for his eyes and jerks back. I prick his chest, nudge him back into the bedroom.

'Good boy, Ezi.'

He's naked but I got to watch him every second. His body's rippling and he's ready for a fight. He'll have a knife somewhere in here, maybe a gun. He'll be looking for a chance to snap it. His eyes flick over to the cabinet.

OK, it's in there. Gun probably. Got a feeling it's a gun.

Prod him back onto the bed.

Black girl cowering in the corner. About fifteen. Starko like him. Clutching a pillow to her chest. I give her a nod.

'You might want to go.'

She looks at Ezi. He takes no notice. He's got his eyes on me.

I ease him onto his back, one knife on his throat, the other on his jack. He's breathing hard but he's fixing me, trying not to show he's choked. The girl hasn't moved. I stab some more words at her.

'Get your clothes on and piss off!'

She scuttles round the bed. I check her quick, just a glance, then back. Can't take my eyes off Ezi for long. But she's a muffin, no sweat, breathing hard as she fumbles on her kit. I call out to her.

'And don't bother looking for Spit, sweetheart. Or anybody else. Time they get here, I'm gone.'

I lean closer to Ezi.

'And this guy's dead.'

Sound of running, front door opening, closing.

More running.

Down the corridor, down the stairs.

Silence.

Just me and Ezi. Him looking up, me looking down. He speaks, low voice.

'You know what I regret?'

I don't give him an answer. He's not waiting for one.

'Cutting up your back,' he goes on, 'and then letting you get away. Before we could rip up your front as well.'

He croaks out a laugh.

'But maybe there's still time.'

'I don't think so, Ezi.'

I fret the blades, just a bit, so he feels 'em. He stiffens.

'So what's this?' he breathes. 'Payback?'

'Kind of.' I fret the blades again. 'Only not for you.'

'Meaning?'

'I got bigger fish than you. And you got bigger fish than me.'

I watch him for a moment, then jump back off him. He stares up at me, not moving. I watch him for a moment, then whip back the knives. He flinches, half-curls up. I reach out, hold the blades over him. Then drop 'em on the bed beside him.

Step back.

Wait.

He straightens, sits up. Got his eyes hot on my face. I know what's coming and it happens quick. He snacks the blades, jumps up, rams his arm into my chest, pounds me back against the wall, knives nicking my throat. His voice comes rasping over me.

'Do it!' he roars. 'Do it, you shit!'

'Got no weapon, Ezi.'

'You must have. Knife, gun, whatever. Something in your coat.'

I shake my head.

'Only weapons I got, you got. In your clammy little hands.'

His face darkens. He shoves his bulk closer, squeezes it against me. He's still angry, still confused. And he doesn't believe me about the weapons.

'I told you,' I murmur. 'I got bigger fish than you. And you got bigger fish than me.'

'Like who?'

'Like the bastards scumming your people. And the big man at the top.'

'We already know them guys.'

'You don't know half of 'em. And you don't know the nob pulling their strings either. I reckon Nelson would be quite interested to know a bit about that. In fact, he'd be dead grateful to you for telling him. So would some of your other brethren. Like Fitz. Or Jimmy-Joe Spice.'

'They ain't brethren.'

'They will be. When they find out the same bums are scumming them too.'

More footsteps on the stairs, pounding close. Didn't take long. I knew the girl would shunt me. Door crashes open and here's the grit. Same age as Ezi but twice the size. I give him a wink.

'How you doing, Spit? Took your time getting here, didn't you?'

He stops, takes everything in, snarls at Ezi.

'Gimme them knives.'

Ezi's watching, still unsure. Spit doesn't wait. Beefs over, makes a grab for the blades. Ezi shifts, keeping 'em back. Spit glares at him, pulls out his own knife, lunges at me.

I let it come. Got to play this right. Split-second to stay, split-second to dodge. Got to let Ezi make his choice. If he will. He does, just in time. Reaches out, grabs Spit's wrist, checks the thrust. Knife's an inch from my heart.

Spit growls at him.

'Let go, man. I got to finish this shit.'

Ezi holds on.

'Not yet. Plenty of time, yeah?'

Spit stares at him for a moment, then at me. And smiles.

'Sure,' he drawls. 'Plenty of time. No rush.'

Yeah, Bigeyes. I know what's ticking his brain. And

I'll tell you something else. I remember that smile. He had it when the two of 'em cut up my back. I saw it when I was facing 'em. And when they spun me over onto my front, and stuffed my face in the mud, and set to work with their blades, I still felt it.

The smile.

Leering down at me.

Even as I screamed.

I force a smile back.

'Trim me up again, Spitty, and you're dead. Want to know why? Cos too many people know about you. I made sure of that. I'm not stupid, OK? I left details. About you and Ezi. And all your little activities. Only reason you're not lemon peel is cos I said you could be useful. So watch your step. And you might just live.'

Spit doesn't answer. But he moves closer. I narrow my eyes.

'I could have taken Ezi out just now.'

'Why didn't you?' says Ezi.

'Yeah, why didn't I?' I fix Ezi again. 'Interesting question. So get this jerk out of my space and we'll talk.'

'You said you was after bigger fish.'

'I said get this jerk out of my space and we'll talk.'

I wait, keep my eyes on Ezi. Feel Spit take a step back. I glance over, look him up and down. Knife's still tight in his grip. I hold out a hand to Ezi.

'I'll have my two back.'

'You reckon.'

'Yeah, I do reckon. You don't need 'em. You got a gun in that drawer.'

Ezi looks over his shoulder at the cabinet, turns back.

'How did you know that?'

Jesus, Bigeyes. Some dronks are piss-thick.

'Never mind,' I say. 'Give me the knives. Go get your gun if it makes you feel safer.'

He doesn't move. But he gives me back the knives. I feel Spit brace himself. Give him a smile, stick the knives back inside my coat.

'OK, boys. Let's deal.'

They stand back, but just a bit. Spit's staying between me and the door. He wants to kill me so bad. And rip me over first. Ezi's still mad too. They're holding back, both of 'em, cos they think I might have something. And they're worried I might not be bluffing about putting their names round, having nebs who'll come looking for 'em.

But they're still seething.

I got to act cool and talk chuck.

'OK, turn the television off.'

'What for?' says Ezi.

'Cos it's making a bloody row.'

'I like it on.'

'Turn it off.'

He fixes me, glances at Spit, back at me.

'We're wasting time,' I say. 'Turn the thing off.'

Ezi doesn't move. Spit grunts, then bustles off into the lounge. I follow him out of the bedroom, Ezi close behind. Spit turns off the television, straightens up, sees the broken glass on the carpet.

'What happened to the balcony door?'

'Our little friend,' says Ezi.

I think of the money in my pocket. More than I should be carrying into a hole like this. I got to play things right and I got to act quick. Ezi's angry already and I don't want him worked up even more about the balcony door. But slipping him jippy won't help. It'll just make him dig into me for what I'm carrying.

Got to move this on fast.

'Yeah, sorry,' I mutter. 'Couldn't think of a better way in.'

I look quickly round the room.

'I need some paper and a pen.'

'Is this a joke?' says Spit.

Yeah right, Bigeyes. Can't imagine these slugs writing, can you?

'Paper and a pen,' I tell him. 'Got to write some stuff down.'

'Just tell us what it is,' says Ezi.

'You won't remember.'

'Try us.'

They're moving closer again. They don't believe me. I got to watch my step or everything'll split.

'I got names you want,' I say. 'Big names. Names Nelson's going to want to know about.'

'We can remember names,' Spit mutters.

'Not this many. And it's not just names. It's places where you'll find 'em. And more. Stuff you won't remember. I need paper and a pen. Wait here.'

I head for the balcony door.

Spit steps in front of me, blocking the way.

'Where you going?'

'Next door had a telephone pad. I saw it when I came through.'

'I'll get it.'

His eyes punch into mine.

'You don't move.'

He glances at Ezi, lumbers out onto the balcony, climbs over to next door, disappears. Back again a few moments later, pad and pen in one hand, knife in the other. Clambers back into the flat.

Ezi's still standing close. Hasn't gone to fetch his gun, but he's pulled on some trousers and he's watching me cute. Spit hands me the pad and pen. I take it, start writing. Feel 'em move close again, one either side. I look up, check 'em over, look down again.

Write on.

'Now listen,' I murmur, still writing. 'You don't get this for nothing.'

Stop writing. Check 'em over again.

They're closer still.

Watching.

I tear off the first piece of paper.

'Which one of you can read?'

'Bastard,' growls Spit.

Ezi takes the paper, runs his eye down it.

'Don't know these names.'

'You don't, do you?' I lean closer. 'But they know you. And Spitty. And all the creepy-crawlies you hang out with. And not only that. They know the rest of your joint. All the way up to Mr Nelson. And they know all about his activities.'

I hold out my hand.

'Give me back the paper.'

Ezi hands it to me. I crumple it up in my fist, throw it over my shoulder onto the floor. Both of 'em stiffen.

'What you do that for?' mutters Ezi.

'Cos you don't need 'em. They're small fry. They're creepy-crawlies too. You can forget about them.'

He won't, Bigeyes. And I don't want him to.

I want Nelson's shades to sort every dronk on that list.

But that's no bum gripe. Ezi'll pick up the list later.

I start writing again. Spit and Ezi close in like before, but not for the same reason. They're craning over my shoulder, reading the names. And now they're interested. You better believe it.

'I know them names,' Spit says.

Course he does. They both do. Every name on the list is a big nob in their world. Small fry in Hawk's world. Just spear-carriers for Hawk. Cos that's what these dronks don't get. To them, Nelson's the top man.

And he's big in his own little pond.

Like Fitz and Spice.

And all the others.

Yeah, there's lots of 'em. Big in their own little ponds.

But Hawk creams the lot. And they never know. Cos they don't even know he exists. All they know is who they meet. The grinks who carry out his work. Some of 'em on that list on the floor. And now, on this other list, a few of the ones higher up.

The spikes.

Not the ones near the top. Nelson's muck doesn't deal with them, doesn't know about them. But these names . . .

I hand Ezi the list. He reads it, holds it out to Spit.

'We know these guys,' he says.

I shake my head.

'No, you don't. You just think you do.'

'We work with 'em.'

'They're scumming you. And they're scumming Nelson. And every bum joint you work with.'

Silence.

Sound of footsteps outside in the corridor, women's voices, low.

Silence again.

'This don't mean nothing,' says Spit. 'It ain't no proof or whatever.'

I tear off several sheets of paper, step back, sit down at the table.

'Now what you doing?' says Ezi.

'This'll take a bit longer. So I'm sitting down.'

They don't move, but I feel 'em watching close. I start writing, slow, careful. Got to get everything right. This all happened over three years ago. Just as well I remember so good. It comes flooding back. Dates, places, everything, like the pen's doing the talking by itself.

Feels funny to be writing.

Even simple stuff.

Never done much writing. Never needed to. Like I

told you, I never went to school. But here's something, Bigeyes. Chew on this. Know who taught me to read and write?

You guessed it.

Hawk.

And here I am, writing words to bring him down. Not that these words will. He's too powerful for anything I can do here. But they'll help. They'll start the fire. Look at 'em, Bigeyes. Tiny little words.

Falling like sparks.

All the scams, all the stings.

Nothing the porkers can use. This is scum against scum. And it won't reach up to the top. But like I say, it'll start the fire. And Hawk'll feel some of the heat.

I stop writing, hold up what I got. Several sheets.

Ezi and Spit come close again, slow.

And I can feel the change in 'em. Yeah, Bigeyes, see the difference? They're thinking, let him write it all out, give us what we want. Then take him out.

I shake my head.

'Taking me out won't help you one bit. Cos I'm not giving you all the information here. Read that. Go on. Read it.'

Ezi takes the sheets, starts to read. Spit doesn't. He's watching me.

Eyes hard.

'It's all there,' I murmur. 'Everything you want. Every scam, every little trick. Every enemy you got and never knew you had. How do I know all that? Cos I was part of it. You hate me cos I took out some of your tribe. But I'm nothing in all this, just like you're nothing. Nelson's been stitched a hundred times and he doesn't even know it. And the scumbos on that list are the ones responsible. The ones he thought were his friends.'

Ezi goes on reading.

Spit goes on watching.

Comes over. Stands by the table, looking down.

I stare up at him, then past at his mate. Ezi finishes reading, comes over. Looks down too. And it's still there, Bigeyes. In their faces. What they want. I speak, slow, clear.

'So here's the deal.'

They don't answer. Just watch. Ezi's clutching the paper tight. His other hand's squeezing into a fist. I think of the knives in my coat. Don't want to use 'em.

I need these dronks alive. Killing dregs won't touch Hawk, won't even brush his brain.

'So here's the deal,' I go. 'You got this information. Nelson's going to want it. So are Fitz and Spice and all the others. Cos it affects them too. Now listen. Nelson's getting all this from me. And in return . . . '

'Yeah?' says Ezi.

I pause, hold their eyes.

'In return . . . Nelson, Fitz, and Spice keep their people off my back.'

'Deal,' says Ezi.

It won't be, Bigeyes. Course it won't. Gangster bosses like Nelson and the other two would never honour such a deal. They'll take the information I've given 'em and still want me dead. I've turned over too many of their dronks to make 'em like me. But that's cute. I wasn't looking for protection. Not really. Just pretending I was. I want 'em to have the information. So they can use it.

And that's it.

And they got to have it this way. They wouldn't take it otherwise, wouldn't trust it, not even from your normal grass and certainly not from me if I just offered it without wanting something back. But give 'em a deal to slap down and they're sweet as pie. But that's just the easy bit done.

Now's the hard part.

Getting out of here.

I stand up.

'There's four more names,' I say. 'The big ones. I'll phone 'em through to you in half an hour.'

'Give 'em now,' says Spit.

I square up to 'em. They're standing firm, blocking my way.

I think of the knives again, feel 'em inside my coat, hard against my sides. I narrow my eyes, lower my voice.

'Kill me and you don't get the juice.'

They don't speak. I go on, slow.

'You got most of the goods. Plenty to get on with. But not the big stuff. The really big stuff. The top four names. I'll give you those when I'm safe out of here.'

Spit's face darkens. I whisper at him.

'Yeah, big guy, you want to screw 'em out of me so bad, don't you? And you know what? You might even manage it. But think for a moment. What if I don't talk? Cos I just might not. And then what? Cos remember what I said. There's bigger fish for all of us. Much much bigger. So ask yourself the question. What's Nelson going to say when you lose the top guys just for the pleasure of dicking me?'

I pause.

'Specially when you know that if Nelson doesn't plug you, my friends will. When they catch up with you later.'

Spit's jaw twitches, falls still. I glance at Ezi.

'What's your mobile number?'

He doesn't answer.

'Ezi.'

'What.'

'What's your mobile number?'

He shrugs.

'I'll write it down.'

'Don't bother. Just tell me.'

'But—'

'Just tell me. I remember numbers.'

Spit's jaw twitches again. Ezi mumbles the number, like he doesn't want me to hear. But I catch it, stick it in my head.

'Step aside,' I say.

They don't. They just watch me, hard, angry.

'Step aside,' I snarl.

They go on watching. Then slowly step aside.

I walk between 'em, over to the door of the flat, open it, look back.

Slip away.

Down the corridor, down the steps, fast as I can, soft as I can. Got to wig it quick, but not so they hear me blasting out. No time to spill though. They'll be having second thoughts, maybe ringing round right now to clan up.

Place could be surrounded before I hit the ground floor.

But there's nobody.

Not yet. Just a couple of trolls slumped by the door. Sound of voices outside, but it's kids. I stop, take a breath, push out into the courtyard. Three boys chipping up at me. Look about eleven.

'What you staring at?' says one.

I don't stop. There's danger round here. Too much, too close. I can feel it. Boy blags off at me again.

'Wanker!' he jeers.

Gives me the finger, giggles to his mates.

Jesus, Bigeyes. I want to whip out the knives, nick his ears. Does he know how many nebs I'd killed by the time I was his age? Obviously not, cos he's still smirking at me.

Shadow over to the right, behind the bins.

Another further back. And I'm sensing more.

Might be nothing to do with Ezi and Spit. There's gangs and gangs round here. But I'm not waiting to find out. Out of the gate, over the street, through the estate.

Checking round, cute as I can. I'm not worried about the younger dronks. It's the big boys I'm bombed about. We're not talking about teen gangs, Bigeyes. We're talking about what teen gangs want to grow into.

There's bad shit out there. Nelson's got some of it working for him. And he's not the only gangster bojo. Fitz and Spice you've heard of, but there's more. And here's something.

Not one of 'em's heard of Lord Haffler-Devereaux. You cracking this?

Not one of 'em.

If anyone's heard of him, it's as a public benefactor. Nothing to do with their pimping and pushing. They'll know some of his spikes. The bastards they thought were allies, the ones I've just blotched on. But they won't know who's at the top.

Playing 'em to death just for fun.

And they're not the only nebs who don't know about Lord H.

Society doesn't know either. Some nebs will have heard of him—aristos mostly, or political toffs, or business bums—but only as a saint. Someone the world can trust. I mean, you couldn't give that much money to charity and not be a saint, now could you?

I'll tell you something, Bigeyes.

If there's genius in evil, he's got it.

Cos here's what's clever: you got all these gangster pods ripping round the Beast, each with its own bojo in charge. And they're all the same. The bojos, I mean. Jumped-up little dictators who think they're big shots cos they've creamed some frosty money and haven't got caught yet.

And cos they got zip loads of trash like Ezi and Spit

to screw stumps if anyone gets in the way. Yeah, they're all the same. But here's the thing: you got all these bojos and their joints scrapping on the same patch, and all that jippy coming in from drugs and sex and all the other shit, but somehow nobody's noticed that the money they're raking in all ends up trickling to the same place.

Hawk's nest.

That's right. The jippy ends up in the hands of a man they don't even know they're working for and haven't even heard of. And what does he use it for? Not drugs, that's for sure. Or sex. Or anything the bojos and their crushers fight over. No, he's got a much higher purpose.

Terror.

That's right.

And why? I told you already.

The Game.

That's what the money's for. That's what the terror's for.

Wrecking.

Economies, businesses, lives, whatever. It's about waiting, hitting, moving in, taking over. This is a war,

Bigeyes. Might not look like one but it is. For Hawk and his fellow slime.

I don't know what they want. Not in detail. Could be anything. But I told you before, it's global. And it's about change. And that means destruction on a massive scale. That's why they're hitting finance. Creating instability. Supporting factions around the world. Whatever's needed.

And there's one thing they really like.

Oh yeah. Yummy yummy.

Arms.

What kind of arms? How high do you want to go? All the way to the top? OK, let's go there. Cos that's how high Hawk wants to go. As high as it gets. So Christ knows who the slimeheads are talking to. All I know is, sooner or later, someone's going to sell 'em what they want.

And then you'll know it's a war.

End of the estate, past the shop, round the corner. Smelly bumping down. Number 17. Check the passengers, jump on, seven stops, off again. Over the road, through the cemetery, into the park.

Stop by the monument.

Check round.

Looks safe. Young mum with a pram. Ancient gobbo on the bench, smoking a roll-up. Couple of dog walkers. Check again, cute as I can. Pull out the mobiles I got left. Not working.

Half-expected it. Drop 'em on the ground, back of the monument, out the gate, down the street to the supermarket. Check faces, in through the door. Might as well make it two birds with one stone while we're here.

And Christ, I'm hungry.

Sandwiches, apples, sausage rolls, bottle of mineral water. Back for more sausage rolls. Checkout. Girl's looking me over, quizzical. But she keeps quiet. Hand her a note, snap the change, out of the supermarket, over to the payphone across the street.

One coin'll do. Cos I'm not saying much.

Dial, wait. Voice grunts into my ear.

'Yeah?'

Ezi's not big on social skills.

'Got something to write with?' I say.

'No. We lost the pen and paper.'

'Well, find something.'

Sound of muttering. I check the street. Two gobbos walking towards the supermarket. Suits. Might be muffins, might be grinks. Hard to tell. Not looking my way. But I don't like the smell of 'em. Ezi comes back.

'I got a pencil.'

'Got some paper or something?'

'I can write on the wall.'

I'm still watching the gobbos. They've stopped. One of 'em's fixing me from the other side of the road. Other's pulled out a mobile. Check round. If they're grinks, there'll be more close by or these two would be over by now.

But there's nobody. Nobody I can see anyway.

'Write this down,' I mutter. 'Lord Haffler-Devereaux.'

'Eh?' says Ezi.

I spell the name for him.

'Who the hell's Lord Haffler-Devereaux?' says Ezi.

'The biggest name on your list. Tell Nelson. Tell everybody. You got no bigger enemy than him. I got to go now.'

'But where's the bastard hang out?'

'Look him up. You'll find him easy. I got to go.'

The gobbos are moving across the street. Heading straight here. Ezi moans at me.

'What about the other names? You said there was four.'

'I was lying. There's only one. But he's enough.'

I kill the phone, step out. Gobbos have spread apart. No question who they are now. But these two aren't the danger. That's going to come from somewhere else.

Don't ask me how I know.

Got it.

Other end of the street.

Two more, closing in.

Back into the supermarket, past the checkouts, down the first aisle. Glance round. Two of the gobbos crunching after me. Step round the shoppers. Old dunny in the way, pushing her trolley.

'Mind out!' she splutters.

Jig round her, on towards the far end of the store. Emergency exit.

Bang through, outside. Collection depot. Couple of

vans, two drivers leaning out the windows, naffing. Check round. Gobbos barging on, one muttering into his phone.

Round the corner, back towards the street. Still clutching the bag of food. Sound of footsteps behind, slamming on the pavement. I got a head start but it's not much, and the other two'll show any moment.

Unless I get to the street first.

I do, just.

But the grinks are close behind. And here's their mates, belting in from the right. Down the street, back the way I came. If I can just get to where I was aiming, I'll be safe for a bit. But only if I throw 'em off.

Least they can't do much with these shoppers around.

But it won't last. And there'll be more dregs crowding in now these ones have clapped me. Check round. They've slowed down. Close behind but hanging back, trying to look normal, waiting for the moment. Two talking on mobiles.

I catch a smile from one.

A chilly smile.

Yeah, grink. You think you got me.

But not yet.

Cos here's something I want. Post van, door open, engine running. And nice Mr Postie over the road, handing a parcel to the gobbo in the bakery. Run down, bung the supermarket bag on the passenger seat with the letters, jump in, close the door, rev up.

Van shoots off.

Yeah, baby.

Scraggy motor. Sings like a crow. But who cares? Check the mirror. Grinks standing still, watching me go. They know they can't run. Not worth it, not here. But Postie's running. Look at him. Cracking his guts to keep up.

Sorry, mate.

You can have it back soon. I'm not going far.

He gives up, stops, looks round for help.

But now I'm gone. Down the street, left at the end, right at the lights, right again. I'm heading the wrong way, then cutting back the right way. Just to throw off the porkers when Postie tells 'em which way I went.

Don't think he got a glimpse of my face. But someone probably did. So the porkers'll be flooding the area too. Just as well I got a place to hide.

It's not a snug, Bigeyes. No snugs in the Beast. But it's where I was planning to slap it for the next few hours. Till it gets dark.

Past the multistorey car park, round the round-about, over the lights, left at the pub, pull over. Check round. Dronky place, yeah? Who'd want to live here? Terrace houses but they're crumbling, see?

Anyway, come on. We got to move. Got to walk back.

But a different way.

Grab the supermarket bag, out of the van, check the street. Kids at the far end, three gobbos on the bench, looking the other way. Don't think they saw me get out of the van. Can't be worrying anyway. Start to walk off.

Stop.

Back to the van. Check the street again. Don't ask me why I'm doing this. I don't know. OK, I do. I'm cranked about Postie, all right? It's not his fault I creamed his motor. Well, it is. But I don't want him getting stuffed cos of me.

Losing his mail as well as his van.

Reach in, rip out the ignition key, lock the van.

Bend down, drop the key on the ground, up against the inside of the front wheel. And now let's go.

Down the street, round the back of the industrial estate, over the main road, down the alleyway, out the other side. OK, see where we are? Look straight ahead. Recognize that?

The park where I tried to use the mobiles.

Only last time we came at it from the other side. Through the cemetery, remember? There's the monument where I dropped the phones. Wonder if someone's picked 'em up. But never mind that. We won't be checking. I got something else to show you.

Only we got to play stealth now.

And that's hard to do in daylight.

Round the edge of the park. Still quite a few nebs about. Muffins, far as I can tell. Woman walking a poodle, kid on a bike, elderly couple sitting on the bench. Walk on, hood up, face low. Seem to have lost that beanie I had.

Never mind.

We're not far now.

Edge of the park, move slow. Round to the side gate, past it, on to where the kiosk used to be, over the path, into the knot of trees. Check again. Main part of the park's over to the right now. You can still see the monument from here. Just the back. Got it?

Now look to the left.

Kind of a dip, then a few old slabs of stone.

Come with me. And keep low. Cos this is a funny place. Druggies hang around here. It's a shithole for a den but it does keep out the wind. And there's a secret even the needles don't know about.

I got shown it by a duff when I was nine. And he died a year later. So maybe no one else knows about it now. Or hardly anyone. Let's hope so anyway.

Down into the dip, stop, check round. Nobody here. Walk on, slow. Got to pick your way carefully. The slabs are all lumpy, see? And with the trees over-head, you're kind of hidden in a little nook.

Stop again.

Look around you, Bigeyes. This is where the drug-gies sit. You can see some of their wreckage on the stones. Now look again. Forget the crap. Tell me what else you see.

Yeah, yeah. I know what you're thinking. It's just

slabs of stone on top of each other. Well, it's not. Far corner, check it out. There's a gap, see? You can squeeze through that. If you're small enough.

The druggies don't bother with it. Nor do the duffs. Too narrow. And nothing much in there—they think. But this other duff—the one I told you about—he was a skinny bastard. And he showed me what's really inside, if you know how to look.

It's not cute, Bigeyes. But I'll tell you what.

It's useful.

Come on.

Drop the supermarket bag in, squeeze through the gap, ease down, feel for the ledge. This is tough. I'm bigger than I was last time I wriggled in here, and I got pockets bulging too. But here's the ledge under my feet.

I'm in.

Sit down on the hard rock, breathe, wait.

Darkness, darkness.

Wait, keep waiting, let it settle. It does, slow. And now I'm seeing it again. The little closed space. Tiny gap above where we slipped in, chilly chamber below, where we are now. Dead rat in the corner. Cans and bottles and syringes that nebs have dropped through the gap over the years.

And that's it.

Only it's not. Cos there's more.

And this is what the old duff really wanted to show me. But to show you, Bigeyes, we got to crawl. Over there, far end, where the top of the rock pushes down. Going to be a scrape. So you better close your eyes if you freak out in confined spaces.

Slow, slow, nice and slow. Worth it to be safe. And right now there's few places we can call safe. Specially in the Beast with grinks and porkers spilling close. And they will be, Bigeyes. Trust me.

They'll be buzzing this area by now.

Only risk here is if they send dogs.

Let's just hope they don't.

End of the chamber, stop where the rock comes down. Now check it cute, Bigeyes. I know it's hard in the dark, but look it over good. It's not the wall, see? It's an overhang. It looks like it's the end of the wall but it's not. Cos the darkness distorts it.

The rock comes down almost to the level of the floor but there's another gap at the bottom. And you can squeeze under that too. If you do it right.

Push the supermarket bag ahead of me, breathe in, flat on the floor, pull myself under. Never liked this bit. And it was easier when I was smaller. But it's not just about size. It's about how you do it. Halfway through now, bit further, bit further, done. Pull myself out the other side.

And now look.

Another chamber. And a tunnel heading down.

Into the dark.

On, on, down, down. Still cramped, but least it's hands and knees now, not flat on the floor. And it gets better soon. I could probably stay here and be OK, but I still don't feel safe. Not when there's somewhere much better just a short way on.

Two spots in the darkness. Two more.

Just rats.

They skitter up, nose round the bag. I shove 'em off. They disappear down the tunnel. Creep on. And here's the shaft. Tunnel goes a bit further, see? Where the rats just went. But we're climbing down here.

Check it out.

Know what this is? You should have worked it out by now. Well, I'm not telling you. You'll find out any-way in a minute. But we got to climb down first. Don't worry. It's easy piss. Check out those wooden ribs. Plenty of 'em to grab hold of.

And we're only talking about a little climb.

Half a minute and we're done.

OK, I was wrong.

Two minutes. But I haven't been here for a few years, all right? And I'm carrying a supermarket bag. Anyway, check around, Bigeyes.

Another tunnel, much bigger, see? Or higher any-way. Doesn't go very far. And we're not going explor-ing. No point. It's blocked both ends. But check out the shape of the walls. Worked it out now?

Jesus, Bigeyes. You just don't notice stuff.

Well, here's a clue. If I took you down that way for a couple of minutes, you'd find some rusty old tracks running along the ground. They don't join up with anything. They run out just before the tunnel gets blocked off at the other end.

Now you get it, right?

We're in one of the old snakeholes. There's loads of these tunnels under the Beast. Some of 'em have got track, some of 'em haven't. Don't know if any trains ever ran on 'em. Maybe they were just started and never finished.

Most of 'em aren't that secret.

So we can't use 'em.

But this one's a little beauty. And we'll slap it here for a bit.

While we wait for the evening. And what's coming next.

Slump on the ground, back against the wall. Breathe slow, breathe again. Pull the supermarket bag over, dig about for the sausage rolls. More spots in the darkness. More squeakies.

Yeah, boys, you want some of this, don't you?

Well, you can't have it.

I kick out. Hear the rats scuttling away. Don't mind 'em much. Quite like 'em even. When you've dug around with as much scum as I have, rats are nothing. They can hang about here if they want. Long as they don't try and bog my food.

Gulp it down.

God, I'm hungry.

Gulp, gulp.

Squeakies come back, watch. I go on eating, bag clutched on my lap. Finish the sausage rolls, start on the sandwiches. Finish 'em, eat the apples, chuck the cores into the darkness. Drink the mineral water. Bung the bottle away.

Lean back.

Breathe again.

Rats have gone.

Pull out the money from all my pockets, check it over. Put a bit back. Enough to get by. No point carrying all the jippy. Too risky. Could lose the lot in one go. So I'll leave most of it here.

Should be safe enough. Long as the squeakies don't eat it.

Shove the bundle of notes in the supermarket bag, stand up, check the wall. Roll up the bag, wedge it high as I can in a gap in the rock, stand back. Good spot. You can't even see it in the darkness. Unless you're looking for it.

We'll take a chance.

Slump back on the ground.

And now I got to work.

Pull out the paper and pen. Didn't see me take this, did you? When I was with Ezi. That's cos you don't watch, Bigeyes. I told you before. OK, now listen. I got writing to do. Lots of it.

So keep out of my way.

I got to think.

And I got to remember.

Lots of gump.

Write, write, write. Never mind what it is. You'll find out later.

Some of it's what I gave Ezi and Spit. But only a bit.

Write, write.

Hands aching, eyes feel grainy. Scratch 'em, lean back. And there's the little spotty lights again. Just two this time. One squeaky friend. Looks at me. And I look back. Into the darkness

And you know what, Bigeyes?

Suddenly feels like I'm looking back into another darkness. Like it was in the old city. Shit, I miss her. She was a bitch sometimes, but I still miss her. And you know what I miss most from that place?

The little snug I showed you.

The one with all the books, remember? The one with *Treasure Island* and that thing about Nietzsche. And *The Wind in the Willows.* The book I read that night. In the darkness. Cos that's my life, Bigeyes. Darkness.

I read in it. I write in it.

I live in it.

Like Ratty over there.

'Ratty,' I murmur.

And I'm thinking of *The Wind in the Willows* again, and Ratty and Mole, and that bit when Moley goes out and gets lost in the Wild Wood, and the snow comes down, and the voices start whispering all around him.

And he's scared.

Till Ratty comes and rescues him.

I look at the tiny eyes. They go on watching, then disappear. Look down again, write on, on, on, stop. Lean back, pull out the knives, rest 'em on my lap. Think of Becky, Mary, Jaz.

Try to calm down. But it's hard. I can feel my heart blamming away inside me. Squeeze the knives, stare round the dark space. And it's like time's never been, never existed. Cos there's something I didn't tell you, Bigeyes. Yeah, I know. Yet another thing.

I was slumped here three years ago.

Same spot.

Exactly.

And you know what day that was?

The day I left the Beast and ran away. Thinking I'd never come back. Knowing Becky was dead. And that it was my fault. I sat here, staring out, like I'm doing now.

Could be the same moment.

All over again.

Cos nothing's changed. Nothing at all.

Except more nebs have died.

I drop my head, squeeze the knives again. The blades glint in the darkness. I close my eyes, think of what I want. What I must have.

I'm desperate to get started. I want to go now, right now. But I can't. I know I can't. Got to make myself be patient, wait till evening, till it's good and dark up top. But I can't leave it too late either. There's too much to do.

So it's wait, wait, wait. Then move, watch.

And hit the place.

At just the right time.

Only it's the wrong time.

Half seven, the clock says. The one on top of the television. I've been here fifty minutes and still nothing. Suppose I couldn't have known for sure. It was always going to be a guess. But a good guess though. Cos this crapper's a creature of habits.

One of 'em over there in the drinks cabinet.

Check round the room.

Never been in here before. But it's what I expected. A living room that's not lived in. One set of curtains drawn back, other set drawn across. Don't ask me what that means. All I know is it's dark and the heating's off and it's getting late.

Eight o'clock, quarter past.

Click of the front door.

I tense up. Hall light goes on. Stabs under the living room door. Feel my way along the wall. Cough on the other side of the door. Sound of post being slit open, dropped on the hall table. Footsteps heading this way.

I edge behind the door.

It opens and the shadow walks in. I slip up behind, whip both knives over the throat. The figure stiffens, holds still. We stand there, quivering against each other. He speaks, low voice.

'There's thirty people you could be.' He takes a slow breath. 'But only one I was expecting tonight.'

I sniff.

'There's more than thirty dronks want a piece of your face, Bannerman.'

'Lucky for me you're not one of them.'

'Sure about that?'

'I think so.'

'Want to find out?'

I move the blades up and down his throat.

'What do you want?' he mutters.

'I've come to deal.'

'Knives won't help you do that.'

'I think they will.'

He grunts.

'They'll only help you if you're prepared to use them. And I don't think you are any more.'

I rasp 'em over his skin, one either side, fix 'em on the carotid arteries. Feel him swallow. I lean closer, murmur into his ear.

'But you don't know for certain, do you, Pugface? You can't be sure. I mean, no one can. Even I can't. That's what's scary. Maybe I want to give up the knife but I got no power to stop myself. Cos it's part of me. Like you and your drinks cabinet.'

'It's empty.'

'No, it isn't.'

'Looked inside, have you?'

'Had to do something while I was waiting for you. And guess what. It's stocked up like you got a regiment coming to stay. Jesus, no wonder you never get promoted.'

Silence. Just the sound of traffic outside the house. And Bannerman's heavy breaths. I keep behind him, blades tight on his neck, check him over. He's staying still, looking straight ahead, watching his step.

He's smart. Trust me, Bigeyes. He might be an alco but he's brained up. Maybe he really was expecting me. I almost believe him. He speaks suddenly, new voice. Kind of conversational.

'Weirdest thing happened today.'

He pauses for a moment, like he's waiting for me to say something. But I don't.

'Boy called Damien,' he goes on. 'Rich kid, super rich. Daddy's got so much money he could practically buy the city. Anyway, Damien gets kidnapped outside his school and taken off in a car.'

I say nothing. Just keep the knives firm on Bannerman's neck. He chugs on, chatty like before.

'Witnesses gave us a fascinating description of the kidnapper. But here's what's strange. Damien gets driven off, then suddenly he turns up again, safe and sound, just an hour or two later. All Daddy can tell us is someone anonymous rang and left a tip-off. And they found the boy in an old garage.'

'What's your point, Bannerman?'

'Just that it's strange.' He pauses again. 'And here's something even stranger. Damien got found just after little Jaz turned up at the police station. Like you told us she would. So obviously, you know, I'm wondering.'

'Wondering what?'

'Whether you know something about Damien too.'

Yeah, Bigeyes, he wants to play games. Well, he's on his own.

'Listen,' I start.

But he cuts in sharp.

'Ever heard of a guy called Pink?' His voice has changed again. More kick. He doesn't wait for an answer. 'Harvey Samuelson Pink. If you want his full name. Owns a chain of casinos and other . . . establishments. Ever heard of him?'

'Might have.'

'He got shot an hour ago.'

I stiffen.

'Coming out of a restaurant,' says Bannerman. 'Died instantly. Big crowd with him. Minders, family, friends. It was his daughter's birthday party, apparently. Two guys on a motorbike. Drove up, three shots into Pink, gone. Nobody else got hurt. So I guess it's pretty clear who they wanted.'

Christ, Bigeyes, it's started quicker than I thought. First name on Ezi's list. Hard to know who cracked it. Nelson's dronks probably. Pink will have been a personal slam for him. But Nelson won't do it all on his own. He'll be naffing with Fitz and Spice.

And the other bojos.

There's going to be blood, Bigeyes. Just wish it was Hawk's too. But it won't be. Not this way. They got his name, yeah, but he'll be too clever for all of 'em. Bringing Hawk down'll take more than two gobbos on a motorbike. Specially now he knows the bojos are on to him.

'So what's this deal?' says Bannerman.

No fear in his voice now. None at all. I still got the knives over his carotid arteries but he sounds almost relaxed. He's even stopped shaking. I got to choke him up a bit or I'll get nothing from him.

I flick the blades, fret 'em on the skin, squeeze a trickle of blood down the left side of his neck. Feel him stiffen again, feel his breathing pump up. Squeeze another trickle of blood, right side. Feel his body go tight.

Wait, watch.

Whisper.

'Now listen good, Pugface. I give you something. You give me something.'

'That's normally how deals work.'

'Don't get clever, Bannerman.'

'What in it for me?'

'Information.'

'What kind of information?'

'Big stuff. Bigger than you can believe.'

'Why give it to me?'

'Cos you're the only person who'll give me what I want.'

He twitches his hands. I don't see it, just feel it. They're loose by his sides but he's kept 'em still all this time. I fret the blades again, let him feel the edges, just a bit. His hands fall still. He takes a long breath, speaks again.

'What is it you want?'

'I want to see Jaz.'

His hands twitch again, fall still.

'Just once,' I say. 'And you know where she is. You got her somewhere safe. I know people are going to take her away soon. Foster parents, whoever. But I'm guessing they haven't taken her yet and I want to see her before she goes.'

'Maybe she's gone already,' says Bannerman.

He's lying, Bigeyes. He's zipping me over. Don't ask me how I know. Testing me to see if I choke.

Jesus, Bigeyes, tell me I'm right.

'She hasn't gone,' I growl. 'Not yet. She's still here. Someone's looking after her. Someone from the police. The foster people haven't come yet. Tomorrow maybe. But not yet.'

It's no good, Bigeyes. I can hear my voice trembling.

And Bannerman will have heard it too.

He waits, like he's playing with me. Then he speaks—and his voice has changed yet again. Like it's softer.

'She's been asking for you.'

I feel myself tense up.

'She's been calling out your name,' says Bannerman. 'Blade, Blade, Blade. Keeps calling for you. And the Jakes girl. Becky.'

'She's called Bex, not Becky.'

'Whatever. Jaz keeps calling for her too.'

'Is Bex with her?'

'No, she's . . . being reunited with her father and stepmother.' A pause. 'Her father's a senior police officer. But maybe you know that.'

I tense up again. I can't handle this, Bigeyes. Got thoughts and feelings flooding me. Can't get my head straight. Can't get anything straight. Got to focus on Jaz. She's what I came here for. And I got one chance to see her before they take her away.

Don't mind what happens after that. Long as she's happy. That's all that counts. Doesn't matter about me. But I want to see her, I got to see her, one more time.

I tighten the blades over Bannerman's throat.

'I want to see Jaz,' I breathe. 'Just me and her alone. And I want you to fix it. Right now. No tricks, no arrest, nice and simple. I see Jaz. You get your information. And I walk free. That's the deal. OK?'

Another silence. A long one.

Then he moves.

Fast.

I'm quick—Jesus, I'm quick—but he slams me like a scud. Before I can plug him, he's got both my wrists clamped in his hands, then the knives wrenched out, and now he's turned, holding 'em both, and he's facing me, eyes bright and fixed.

I take a step back, feel the wall behind me. Bannerman kicks the door shut, moves closer, stops. Leans down.

'Deal,' he murmurs.

Then hands me back the knives.

'Let's go,' he says.

We don't talk in the car. Not a word. I watch the streets slip by. Nebs crowding everywhere: bars, cafés, clubs, restaurants. Porkers spilling round. Grinks too, probably.

Only I don't see 'em.

Cos I don't care. I'm hardly watching. Not right now. Maybe they'll clap me, maybe they won't. Don't give two bells. I got one thing in my head. That's all.

I'm going to see Jaz.

I think.

Cos here's the thing. Bannerman could be lying. Might just be driving me to the police station. Taking a dronky route if he is, but that could be part of the rip. To sting me into thinking he's cool when he's not.

And I wouldn't blame him. Shunting me, I mean. I'd probably do the same if I was him. Multiple murderer, the kid everyone's looking for, and here he is blobbed in my car. I'd take the little shit straight in.

Only Bannerman's different. That's why I'm taking the risk. I mean, he might be an alco and a sad git, but he's a good porker. And he might just be an honest one.

I glance at him. Got his lips tight together.

'Struggling, aren't you, Pugface?'

'Over what?'

'Handing me in. Or not.'

'Not struggling over that,' he mutters.

'What, then?'

He bungs me a look.

'I'm struggling over whether I'd take someone like you to see a three-year-old daughter of mine.'

He looks back at the road, drives on. Left at the junction, down to the traffic lights.

Red.

We stop, wait.

Rain starts to fall. Hard, gobby drops. Bannerman watches 'em. Hard, gobby eyes. Flicks on the wipers. Lights change. He drives on. First right, second left. Pulls over. I check out the street.

Residential.

Good start. Not a porker joint in sight. But it might still be a trick. Bannerman turns off the engine, twists round in the seat, frowns at me.

'Still not sure why I'm doing this.'

'Maybe you just like me, Pugface.'

'I don't like you and you don't like me. So let's jump over that bit. This information you say you've got—'

'Afterwards.'

'I'm going to need some proof of—'

'Afterwards.' I fix him. 'When I've seen Jaz. And you've let me out again. That's when you get your information.'

'How do I know you'll give me anything?'

'You don't.'

He watches me, narrowed eyes. Then reaches for the car door.

'Wait here.'

'No tricks, Bannerman.'

'Get a life.'

He climbs out of the car, cuts over to number seven. I check the house quick. Two lights on upstairs, one downstairs. I'm guessing there's one porker in there, Fern if I'm lucky. If there's more than one, I got to think again.

He rings the bell, waits.

No answer. I watch, cute as I can. This could go badly wrong. He didn't phone or text ahead. I know that. I've been checking him close ever since we left his house. So whoever lives here doesn't know I'm coming. But I still don't like it. There could be Christ knows how many nebs in that house. And maybe not Jaz at all.

Shadow appears in the glass of the door. I relax a bit. It's a figure I recognize. A bosomy figure. Door opens. And there's DI Fern.

Looks a lot older than the last time I saw her. But that was years ago. Still got plenty up top. And I don't mean her head. Though I'm guessing she's well stitched there too.

Bannerman beckons her out into the street. Another good sign. They haven't gone inside to talk. He's keeping her where I can see 'em, spite of the rain. But I'm still nervous.

I got pictures of Jaz buzzing my head now. They're banging my mind so bad I want to forget everything, dump the risk, jump out of the car, charge in. I'm so close to seeing her again. I can feel it.

But I got to be patient, make myself wait. Cos even if I do go crashing in, what'll that do to Jaz? I scared her once before, scared her terrible. And she's been scared terrible already. I got to hold back or I'll make it worse.

But I'm desperate to get inside that house.

Bannerman's coming back.

I climb out of the car, stand there on the pavement. He walks up, stops, looks me over. Rain's still flicking down. I stare back at him. Hard to read his face. Check past him. Fern's still standing in the doorway, watching.

Hard to read her face too.

Bannerman speaks.

'Come on.'

I follow him up to the house. Front door's wide open. I don't trig through. Can't anyway. Fern's blocking the entrance. Check her over. No weapons, no cuffs. Just a dark look on her face.

Whip a glance past her into the house. Hall stretching straight ahead, rooms off it either side, doors closed. Stairs at the end. Nobody else in sight. She speaks.

'Coat.'

Hard voice. Hard as her face.

Holds out a hand.

'Coat,' she says again.

I take it off, hand it over. She doesn't check the pockets. Doesn't move aside either.

Bannerman shifts on his feet. She glances at him, back at me.

'Just a few minutes,' she says. 'That's all you've got.'

Steps aside, nods me into the house. I check her over again, and Bannerman, and the street. Walk in. Hear the front door close behind me. Stop, check 'em again. Both watching me close. I'm watching 'em back too. But most of me's listening.

For danger.

And for Jaz.

No sound of either. Just the grind of traffic outside the house. Nothing but silence in here. Fern reaches to the left, hangs my coat on a hook by the front door, faces me again.

'You can have it back when you leave,' she says.

I don't answer. I haven't thought that far ahead. Leaving, I mean. All I can see is what I want now. As much time as I can get with Jaz. A few minutes, Fern said. Well, I'll take what I get. And after that?

Can't see anything after that.

Maybe I'll get away, maybe I won't. So what do I care about a coat? They'll cream the blades out of it anyway. Course they will. They got to do that. Bannerman knows I got 'em in the pockets. But what does it matter? What does anything matter?

A few minutes with Jaz.

I'll settle for that.

Fern walks slowly up to me, stops. Talks soft. Not friendly. Just soft.

'She's in the room at the end.'

I turn towards it. Brown door, closed. Not a whisper of noise behind it.

Is she really in there, Bigeyes? Cos I'm full of doubts now. And if she is, do you reckon she's listening to all this? Maybe she can't hear us. Fern talked so soft. And I haven't said a word yet.

I want to call out suddenly, shout Jaz's name, tell

her it's me. Tell her I love her. But I know I can't. It's a dimpy idea. It could smash everything. Fern speaks again, soft like before.

'I'm letting you see her for one reason only. Because Inspector Bannerman thinks it might help her. I don't like it and he and I will probably get into trouble for it.'

She frowns.

'But I'm warning you . . . ' She lowers her voice even more. 'If you add one tiny bit more distress to what that little girl has already suffered, then I'll personally—'

'What happened to her?' I mutter.

Fern doesn't answer. Just presses her lips together.

'Tell me what happened to her,' I say.

Bannerman lumbers up.

'We don't know what happened to Jaz.' He's talking as quiet as Fern. 'She hasn't been physically harmed, as far as we can tell.'

'Has she been . . . '

I stop. Can't finish the question. Can't bear to.

But Bannerman answers it anyway.

'She hasn't been . . . interfered with.'

'But she's badly traumatized,' says Fern. 'She's hardly spoken. Just stays silent and closed up, and when she makes any noise at all, it's mostly to cry out in this quiet . . . kind of whimper. And mostly for you. Or Rebecca Jakes.'

I hurry down the hall, stop outside the door, look back. Fern and Bannerman are standing where they were, watching close. I turn back to the door, stare at it.

Jesus, Bigeyes. My heart's pumping. I'm more scared than I've ever been in my life. That's right—scared. Not of what I'm going to find. But of something far worse.

I'm scared I won't be able to make her better again.

I take a breath, reach out, grip the handle.

Push open the door.

Step in, stop. One glance is enough. I close the door behind me. Cos I've seen what I want. And I want it all to myself. She's sitting in the corner of a sofa, curled up, all by herself. No one else here. Just me and Jaz.

Looking at each other.

She's got her eyes wide and she's staring. Not talking, not murmuring or whimpering or crying. Just staring, like I'm . . .

I don't know.

Just staring.

She moves, a little shiver of her arm. It's clutching a cuddly thing. Teddy or a squirrel, I think. Can't see cos it's tucked under her. Some part of me's checked out the rest of the room. Window facing the garden. Bookshelves, desk, armchair.

Nothing that matters.

Cos only one thing matters.

'Jaz,' I murmur.

I'm standing like I'm frozen. I don't know how to move, how to make her not be scared. Cos she is scared, Bigeyes. And I can see now what her eyes mean. They're looking for new danger. Cos that's all she's seen since those dronks took her.

And plenty before too.

'Jaz, it's me, baby.'

She squeezes the cuddly thing closer. And now I'm moving. I'm walking over, slow as I can, trying to smile. She's still staring, wide eyes, and now her mouth's opening. I can feel the scream inside it, ready to break out.

I got to stop it.

Or Fern'll smack me straight out of here.

'Jaz, sweetheart,' I whisper.

The scream doesn't come. She's still got her mouth open but she's just watching. I drop down on my knees. I'm close to the sofa now and I can reach her. I stretch out my hand, see her edge back.

'It's all right, Jaz.'

She holds still, fixes my hand with her eyes, watches it draw near.

'It's all right, Jaz. It's me.'

She pulls out the cuddly thing, stuffs it against her chest, holds it tight.

'Squirrel Nutkin,' I murmur.

I stop my hand. Jaz doesn't speak, just goes on watching me.

'I read about Squirrel Nutkin,' I whisper. 'In one of my snugs. And Peter Rabbit. Do you remember him? You used to have a cuddly Peter Rabbit. I carried him for you once. What happened to him?'

She doesn't answer, doesn't show any sign she's understood.

'I must have dropped him somewhere,' I say.

I reach out, stroke the squirrel.

'But you got a better friend now.'

I hear footsteps outside the door. Two sets. They stop. I wait, still watching Jaz, Jaz still watching me. Door doesn't open. But the footsteps don't start again. I can feel Fern and Bannerman out there, listening.

I got to keep 'em out.

Cos I'm telling you, Bigeyes, I won't get this moment back. And there won't be another one after it. I got to talk, make 'em hear something. If there's silence, they'll come bursting in.

'Do you remember that story, Jaz? The one I made up for you?'

Not a word from her. She just clutches the squirrel and stares. I feel Fern and Bannerman fidget outside the room. I hurry on.

'It was a story about Mr Bunny. And this little girl called Jaz. And I never finished it for you. Do you want me to finish it for you now?'

I look at her face. Not even sure she's hearing me. I ease myself onto the sofa, sit still. She doesn't pull back, just goes on staring like before. Again I hear 'em fidget outside the door.

I reach out my hand, slow as I can. Jaz watches it come near, and there's that scream ready in her mouth again. It's in her eyes too. I stop my hand, rest it on Squirrel Nutkin.

'It's all right, Jaz. It's all right. I'm not going to hurt you. I'll never ever do that. I'm just going to sit here and—'

'Blade,' she murmurs.

Her voice chills me. I wasn't expecting her to speak. I was expecting her to scream. I'm still expecting her to scream.

'Blade,' she murmurs.

'That's right, baby. I'm Blade.'

She goes on speaking my name. Soft little voice, no expression. Like it's just a sound she's making, a sound with no meaning. And suddenly it's like the name's lost its meaning for me too. She's just saying it, soft, slow, like it's a little piece of noise.

That's all.

BLADE

She doesn't know what a blade is. So she's just making a noise. Not even sure she connects the word with me. But I'm wrong. Look at her face, Bigeyes. There's so much in there I can't see. But there's also something I can't miss.

Myself.

Locked in her face.

Locked in my name.

And now in her voice.

'Blade,' she murmurs. 'Blade, Blade, Blade.'

I pull her close, all in one movement, and she bundles into me like it's all she ever wanted. I'm crying now, can't stop it. She's not. She's just closed up inside my arms, quiet again. Stopped talking, just breathing, resting against me.

And I'm going on crying.

Silent too. Not wailing or calling out, just . . .

Crying.

Like my whole life's seeping out of my eyes.

She must feel it. My whole body's shuddering. She's got to know I'm breaking up. Cos I am, Bigeyes. I'm breaking up. There's no part of me left that's whole any more.

I stiffen suddenly.

Door bell just rang. I definitely heard it. And now footsteps outside, heading down the hall. Jaz takes no notice. Just goes on cuddling up. I stroke her hair, her beautiful, beautiful hair.

'Jaz,' I'm whispering. 'Beautiful Jaz.'

But I'm listening too. Sound of the front door opening. Bannerman's voice, then Fern's. Don't catch the answer. But I hear the front door close, then footsteps again.

More than last time.

Lots more.

I breathe slowly out. So it was a trap after all. I half-expected it. Check round the room. I could wig it out the window. Into the garden and round the side of the house. Might get away. But I don't move.

And you know what, Bigeyes?

I never intended to.

Cos all I want's here.

'Little flower,' I whisper to her. 'Just like Becky. Too good for a shit like me.'

She looks up at me suddenly. Like it's a reproach.

'Jaz,' I murmur.

I lean down, kiss her on the forehead, straighten up. She goes on watching me, then turns to face the door.

Cos it's just opened.

And there's a small girl looking in.

About Jaz's age and she's standing there all by herself. Nice-looking kid, shy but friendly. Chestnut hair, brown eyes. Not looking at me.

Looking straight at Jaz.

And Jaz is looking back.

I go on holding her. Sound of rain pattering against the window. The little girl in the doorway flicks a glance behind her—and a hand appears, reaches down, strokes her head.

A woman's hand.

I feel Jaz shift against me, twist round to look better. I don't stop her. Cos I know what's happening now, Bigeyes. It's not a trap. It's something worse.

It's the moment I lose Jaz for ever.

There's nebs out there. I can't see 'em all but I can feel 'em. And I know exactly who they are. Maybe Jaz does too. She's sitting up, staring towards the door, and she doesn't look scared.

Maybe it's the other girl who's making her feel that.

Hope so.

Yeah, it is.

I can tell. They like each other. Both shy, both a bit wary, but they're cute with each other. Long way to go. Yeah, yeah. But who cares, long as it works out. The rest are coming in.

Woman, man, boy about five. Got to be the little girl's brother. Same kind of face, same kind of shyness. It's in the parents too. There's something quiet about 'em, something polite and respectful.

I like these nebs.

Woman bends down, takes her little girl's hand, smiles at Jaz.

'Hello, Jaz,' she says.

Jaz doesn't answer. Woman doesn't seem flummed. Just goes on smiling. Husband comes in with the boy. Tall gobbo, lanky. Takes the boy's hand, bends down next to his wife and the girl.

Smiles at Jaz too.

I feel her move in my arms. She's not pulling away but she's not tucking close either. I don't know what she's feeling, Bigeyes. I can't crack it any more. But I do know one thing.

I know what I got to do next.

I slip my arms from her, edge back against the sofa.

She looks round at me suddenly. I fix her back and smile too, best I can. Her eyes trig over me. She doesn't smile, just watches. I lean down, kiss her again on the forehead.

'I'm Sophie,' says the woman.

I look up, realize she's talking to me.

'This is my husband Rory,' she says.

The gobbo gives me a nod. The woman motions to the kids.

'This is my daughter Melody. And my son Philip.'

I look round at 'em all.

'And you are?' she says.

I see Fern and Bannerman standing in the doorway. Watching me. Message clear.

I look back at the woman.

'I'm a friend of Jaz,' I answer.

I stand up, walk over to the door. I don't look back. But I'm waiting for a sound, praying for a sound. A whimper, a word. My name again. Anything from Jaz.

But she's silent.

I reach the door, stop, look back.

She's watching me, just me. I feel my mouth move, feel Jaz's name whisper inside it. But no sound comes out. The woman called Sophie leans closer to the sofa, reaches out to Squirrel Nutkin.

'You've got a fluffy friend, Jaz,' she says.

She strokes the furry head.

'Melody likes Squirrel Nutkin.'

Jaz takes her eyes from me, looks over at the girl.

And I slip out of the room.

Down the hall towards the front door. I can see the rain streaming down the glass, dark against the night outside. Fern and Bannerman stay close, one either side of me. I don't look at 'em. All I can see is the rain on the door.

Gushing down the glass like the tears on my face.

I don't care if Bannerman sees 'em, or Fern, or anyone. Not now. I hear voices back in the room. The woman's, the boy's, the gobbo's, little Melody's.

Nothing from Jaz.

The rain goes on streaming.

I stop at the front door, reach for my coat on the hook. Fern and Bannerman stay close. They're not blocking the door. I thought they would. But they're staying close. I pull on the coat, feel in the pockets. Knives still there.

I look over at Bannerman.

'You can keep the knives,' he says. 'They're no harm to anyone now.'

'What do you mean?'

'Well, you're never going to use them again, are you?'

I feel the darkness closing over me. It's not the night outside the door. It's the night inside my head. The voices from the room down the hall whisper through it. The rain drums on against the glass. I breathe hard, try to block it all out, but I can't.

Fern speaks. Her voice seems to come from a distant place.

'You asked on the phone about the elderly Irish woman.'

'Mary,' says Bannerman.

He too sounds far away.

I try to speak but I can't. I just see the darkness. And Jaz's face, and Becky's, and now Mary's, all three locked inside it. I know what Fern's going to say. She's going to say Mary's dead.

'She's in a hospice,' says Fern. 'I just heard before you arrived.'

I yank open the front door. Rain slams into my face. The voices down the hall go on. I step into the night, stumble down to the gate. Bannerman catches me up, pulls me round.

'You said you've got information. We had a deal, remember?'

I stare up at him. The rain's blackening his face, like it's blackening everything else. I squeeze the knives in my pockets. Jaz is gone, Becky's gone. In a few short hours, Mary'll be gone too.

What's left for me now?

'Be at your house in an hour,' I mutter.

I turn and blunder off down the street. Bannerman calls after me.

'That won't do!'

'Be at your house in an hour.'

I start to run.

'Running isn't the answer!' he shouts.

I put on speed, pelt through the rain, let the darkness drown me. Bannerman goes on bellowing after me.

His voice is just as angry later. At the other end of the phone.

'You said an hour! What time do you call this?'

'Do you want what I got or not?'

'It's close on midnight, for Christ's sake!'

'Do you want what I got or not?'

I stare out of the phone box. Rain's stopped but it's still wet outside. Wet and cold and dark. Nothing out there worth anything. Nothing in here either.

I crunch in some more coins.

Taken me ages to get here. Had to watch every shadow. And there's lots of 'em out there, more than ever now the blood's starting to run. The bojos are kicking stumps and Hawk'll want something back. And not just from them but from me.

Me more than anybody.

Porkers buzzing too. Same agenda. They all want me, Bigeyes. Every single one. But you know what? I stopped caring. Cos I'm spun. That's right. I got zippo left.

I kept telling myself, as I was ducking my way here, that least I've done one good thing. Got Jaz back, got her safe. But when you think about it, even that's a spewer. I mean, how good was that really? If it hadn't been for knowing me, she'd never have been in danger in the first place.

So my helping her counts for dog shit.

Cos here's what it comes to, Bigeyes. All I've ever done is hurt and kill. And now the things I've done are hurting and killing me back. I guess that's how it works. You give it out, you get it back.

Bannerman speaks again, quieter.

'I want what you've got.'

'Where are you?' I mutter.

'At my house. Like you told me to be.'

'What room are you in?'

'Does this matter?'

'What room are you in?'

Bannerman gives a sigh.

'The hall. I'm standing in the hall.'

'Take the phone into the living room.'

'What for?'

'Just do it, Pugface.'

Another sigh, a sound of walking.

'I'm in the living room. Now what?'

'Go over to the bookshelves.'

'Don't tell me you're into reading.'

Jesus, Bigeyes. If only he knew. But I got no time to naff about books.

'Top shelf,' I tell him. 'Far left. City atlas. Great big thing.'

It is too. But we're talking about the Beast, remember. The atlas is never going to be small. This one's got Christ knows how many pages. All the streets and all the suburbs going out miles.

'Got it?' I say.

'Give me a chance.'

Sound of a clink.

'You drinking, Bannerman?'

He doesn't answer. More footsteps, a grunt.

'I've got the atlas,' he says.

'Open it. Page twelve. Keep the thing flat or the stuff'll fall on the floor.'

'What stuff?'

'Just do it, will you?'

A pause. Another clink.

'And put the bloody glass down.'

He takes no notice. I can hear him knocking back. Pouring another one too. But now he's flicking through the papers from Ezi's notepad that I blobbed inside the atlas when I broke in earlier.

'What is this stuff?' he says.

'Read it. I'll phone you back in a few minutes.'

'Hold on. Where are you?'

'Never mind.'

'Give me your number. I'll ring you back.'

'No, I'll phone you.'

'But—'

'Read, you bastard.'

I hang up. Bit of a chance. He might get the porkers tracking the call. But I'm hoping he's too busy reading. I'll give him some time. He needs to take this in. And I need time too. Yeah, Bigeyes. I'm in a bad state.

Got to clear my head somehow, calm down, stay

strong. Cos the darkness is still there, outside, inside, everywhere. I go on checking shadows up and down the street.

Muffins so far. Duffs and drunks mostly.

But what about the shadows moving in my head? They're not muffins. I'm telling you, Bigeyes, they're meaner than the meanest grink.

I hope he's reading. Christ, he better be. Trouble is, I kept him waiting for this call, cos I couldn't ring him any earlier, and he's got mad. So he probably tipped a few down him while he was slopping round.

I've given him all I got, Bigeyes. Written it all down on those little bits of paper. Names, scams, companies, banks, all the players I can think of, all the deals I know about. How the bojos get shunted, how the jippy gets moved.

And where it goes.

Accounts, numbers, details.

Everything I can remember.

And something else I've written down. My little cupboards in the old city. Like the bridge over the stream, remember? I've told him where they are. Every single one. And I got lots.

I messed up, Bigeyes. Might as well admit it. Made a big, big mistake when I ran away from Hawk three years ago. I should have just wigged it. Blasted out of the Beast and gone to ground far away. He might just have left me alone.

Probably not, cos he's proud.

But he might have done.

Only I screwed up bad. Took stuff from him, took it away with me, cos I was angry and I wanted to hurt him. Small things, easy to carry, but things he really values. Cos they're priceless. Most of 'em anyway.

Something you got to know about Hawk. He likes to possess. Money, power, people—and beautiful objects. Specially if they've been creamed out of someone else's collection. Or even better—lifted from a public gallery.

He loves having original paintings and artefacts in his secret rooms that only he can ever look at. Knowing the porkers and art experts and gallery curators are churning up the world trying to find 'em.

But I didn't take paintings. Too bulky. I took things I could carry easy. Jewels—dodgy, dangerous jewels that cost lives—and miniature sculptures from China and India and God knows where. Ancient parchments, original letters, a lock of Mozart's hair, stuff like that.

Small things, but worth a mint. Wrapped 'em all up proper so they're snug, then stashed 'em in my cupboards, along with jippy I lifted too.

And there's something else I took.

Something Hawk wants back even more than the stuff I just mentioned. I shouldn't have touched it. I know that. But it's too late to give it all back to him now. Even telling him where it is won't save me. I've hurt his pride, done him too much harm, plus I took his kid. So my days are numbered.

But maybe—just maybe—I can do one good thing.

Before the darkness finishes me.

I pick up the phone, ring again. Bannerman answers at once.

'Yes?'

'Have you read it all?'

'Yes.'

I can hear his breathing at the other end of the line. It's fast and jerky.

'Is this stuff for real?' he says.

'Yeah.'

'Are you serious? Lord Haffler-Devereaux?'

'Let's call him Hawk.'

'But he's one of the most—'

'I know who he is. Or who you think he is.'

Bannerman takes another jerky breath.

'And these other names . . . Raven, Swan, Swift, Owl, Condor . . . are you really suggesting they're code names for the people you've written alongside them?'

'Yeah.'

'But these are all—'

'Big hitters in their own countries. I know that. Jesus, Bannerman. Don't you get it?' I squeeze the phone tight. 'This is something global. It's a war. Just cos you don't know about it doesn't mean it's not happening. So go and check what I've given you.'

'You've also written Eagle. But there's no name alongside it.'

'That's cos I don't know who Eagle is. I just know Eagle's the one at the top. Don't know which country. But it's someone very high up. I'm guessing royal or presidential.'

Bannerman grunts.

'None of this is proof. And I can't help wondering how you've got hold of all this information. There's loads of it. You're not going to tell me you've been carrying these notes around with you for three years.'

'I wrote it all down today.'

'From what source?'

'From memory?'

'You can't have done. There's too much.'

'Well, I did. I remember stuff, all right? It's how I am. I notice things and I stack 'em in my head. Like all your phone numbers.'

I stiffen. A figure's stumbling towards the phone box. But it's only a duff. He peers through, makes a face. I give him the finger and he staggers off.

Bannerman comes back.

'OK, OK. Let's pretend you've got this amazing memory. That you notice things and remember them. That Lord Haffler-Devereaux really is the Hawk, and this . . . organization exists. And all the other things on these sheets are true. It still doesn't explain one thing.'

'What's that?'

'How on earth do you expect me to believe that a man as dangerous and clever as Hawk would give you access to such information in the first place?'

I stare out of the phone box into the darkness. The duff's now slumped on the far side of the street, staring down at the ground. A shiver of rain dusts the glass.

I bite my lip, bang in some more coins. Talk into the silence.

'Do you know what it's like to be a slave, Bannerman?'

He doesn't answer. But I don't want him to. I frown.

'It's like having no being. No body, no mind, no will. You're like a puppet. Your master controls every part of you. Tells you when to live. Tells you when to die. And when to kill.'

I spot a new shadow moving at the far end of the street.

But I go on talking.

'Hawk got me when I was seven. I started off as a bit of fun for him. I reckon you know what I mean. But he soon realized I could be useful in other ways. That's how I got close to him. I found stuff out cos he got careless. He had so much power over me he never thought I could be dangerous to him.'

The shadow at the end of the street stops. I watch it, go on.

'He let me right into his life. Even when I was seven. Don't think he realized I remember everything I see and hear. Or pretty much everything. His tongue used to loosen sometimes. He'd wham the crap out of me, then he'd want to talk. In a dronky kind of way, I think he was trying to impress me.'

Bannerman's quiet at the other end of the line.

Can't even hear him breathing.

'Go on,' he murmurs.

'He just treated me like I was no risk to him. And I wasn't. Not then. I was still living wild, cracking it on the streets with low-life. Hawk set me up in dives round the city. I'd live with pushers and pimps and other scum. People he could contact when he wanted me. And he started to want me a lot.'

'So he'd send someone for you?'

'Yeah.'

'Did you ever refuse to go?'

'Once. When I was eight. But it never happened again.'

'What do you mean?'

'Work it out for yourself, Bannerman.'

He says nothing. I go on.

'Hawk owned me. All of me. That's it. He just never saw me as a problem. He'd let me into his private rooms, show me his secret possessions. Let me sit on the floor while he worked at his desk or chummed with his business friends. None of 'em even looked at me. I was just some kind of toy. A mascot. A kid he was whamming. Dangerous to everybody else. But nothing to them.'

I stop. The shadow's moving again. Heading down the street towards me.

Slow.

I watch it, go on talking.

'So I heard stuff, noticed stuff, and remembered it. The passwords he keyed into his computer, the combination of his private safe, stuff like that. I wasn't looking to use it. I just couldn't help spotting it and remembering it. And all the other things he dropped into my head. It stayed there. And when I ran away, I decided to use it.'

'Why?' says Bannerman.

I don't answer. I'm watching the shadow. It's stopped again, halfway down the street. Not watching me. Don't think so anyway. But I'm watching back.

'Why?' says Bannerman.

'Cos I wanted to hurt him.'

Another shiver of rain against the glass. The duff over the street hauls himself to his feet and blunders off. The shadow doesn't move. I feel the darkness draw round me again.

'He got me too early, Bannerman. I was an angry, dangerous little kid but I was vulnerable, and he was too powerful. He could do anything he wanted with me. And you never knew what it was going to be. Sometimes, just for a moment, I'd start to think he cared for me. He'd talk soft, teach me to read and write, whatever. Then he'd whip me just for fun.'

'Jesus.'

'He liked pain. Giving it. Liked seeing me suffer and knowing I'd still be his. He knew I'd do anything for him. And he was right. By the time I was ten, I was his personal assassin.'

I feel the flashbacks start. I close my eyes.

Open 'em again.

'I'd kill anyone he told me to. It was easy at first. No one suspected a little kid. And I could look tiny and sweet and innocent when I wanted to. By the time the target worked out I was dangerous, he was dead.'

More flashbacks. I push 'em aside, hurry on.

'I only ever killed murderers. Hawk's targets were all people who'd killed one of his men. And I was told to settle the score. But then the other crime joints started working me out. And you and your police mates got a bit wise too. Killing got rougher. I was starting to crack up.'

I stop, breathe hard.

Stare at the pictures in my head.

'I kept seeing the faces of the people I'd killed. Every single one. I still see 'em. I get flashbacks all the time. I'm getting 'em now. Their faces peering at me. I tell myself they were all slime anyway, but it doesn't work.'

'Listen,' says Bannerman, 'you've got to—'

'I started to fall apart. Hawk just gave me another

target. I told him I couldn't do it. Tried to run away. Then . . . something else happened . . . '

'What?' says Bannerman.

I stare out at the shadow. It's moving again, down the street towards me. Stops at the alley on the left, turns into it, disappears.

'What?' says Bannerman.

'Look at the last sheet.'

'Eh?'

'Look at the last sheet.'

'It's a list of names,' he says.

'They're the names of the people I've killed.'

'Are you serious?'

'Every one.'

And I've put Paddy down too, Bigeyes. Case you're wondering. But not Lenny and the grunt. Cos I didn't kill 'em, all right? They fell from the balcony by themselves.

But I'm seeing their faces too.

Along with all the others.

'Look,' says Bannerman. 'You've got to come in to the station. You've—'

'Put down the papers.'

'What?'

'Put down the papers. Look inside the atlas.'

'What's this about?'

'Just do it.'

'What page?'

'The page you're already on.'

Silence while he looks. I stare out into the street. Rain's stopped. No shadows moving. Except in my head.

'Have you found it?' I say.

'Found what?'

'Top of the page. Far right.'

'A small cross,' he says. 'Which I presume you drew.'

'It marks a spot at the end of a graveyard. By an oak tree. Get your spade and go dig. You'll find a tin box with an external hard drive inside. It's a backup drive from Hawk's computer. I took it from his safe when I ran away. There's a slip of paper in there too with the passwords you need. So check out the drive. You'll find it interesting.'

And that's the one, Bigeyes. The thing I shouldn't have taken. Tell you why. Cos it kept Hawk on my trail. But you know what? Now I'm glad I took it. Cos this could sink the bastard. Long as Bannerman follows it up.

There's evidence on that backup drive. Maybe all we'll ever get. It's three years old and Hawk'll have changed computers and files and passwords a hundred times since then. But there's enough on that backup drive to incriminate him.

Tell you how I know. Cos there's no way he'd have sent that many grinks after me if it had only been small shit.

'Go dig, Bannerman,' I mutter. 'And do it quick.'

Peeps in the phone.

I push another coin in. Just one. Don't need any more now.

'I got to go,' I murmur.

'Come to the station.'

'There's no point.'

'There is a point. I promise you there's a point.' Bannerman's talking fast, almost gabbling. 'Listen— you've killed. You've killed several times. And you've got to face up to that and take what comes. But you've got a defence. Are you listening to me?'

'Yeah.'

'You've got a defence. You were in someone else's power. It's possible to argue that to a large extent you were forced to act. You've also now given the police valuable information. So there are mitigating circumstances. You must come in.'

I lean against the side of the phone box.

It's no good, Bigeyes. I'm so tired now. And so scared. I stare into the darkness again, search for the faces. But they're not there. Everything's black now. Just one thing left to do.

'Sorry, Bannerman,' I whisper.

I hang up, plod out of the phone box, down the street to the alley. Stop, check it out. The shadow's halfway down, leaning against the wall at the back of the pub. I shuffle down towards it. The figure stiffens as I draw near.

'You're late,' says Ruby.

I stop, peer up into her face.

'Didn't think you'd come,' I say.

'Yeah, you did.' She looks me up and down. 'So cut the crap.'

I turn down the alley, make my way towards Mother Grime. I can see the river even from here. She's glowing in the night where the lights from the shore speckle her sick, black body.

I don't check to see if Ruby's following. I know she is. I can feel it, like I can feel her anger, her hatred. Sound of laughter coming from The Turk's Head on our right.

What is it about laughter from pubs, Bigeyes? Why does it always sound unhappy? Maybe it's just me. Cos I'm unhappy, the sound of nebs enjoying themselves makes me feel worse. Maybe that's it.

But it's not. I know it's not. Some laughter's OK. Yeah, yeah. But I'm telling you. A lot of laughter's a cry for help. Not that I'm laughing. No point. I'm just crying for help.

And there's not much point in that either.

End of the alley, stop, wait for Ruby. She catches me up, stops by my shoulder. I feel her looking at me, hard. I don't look back. I can't. Guilt chokes me up every time I see her face.

I stare out over the main road, then beyond it to Mother Grime.

'Well?' says Ruby.

I nod down to the left.

'Fish and chip shop down there. See?'

'What about it?'

'We used to meet there. Me and Becky.'

Tap on my shoulder. Makes me turn my head. Ruby's staring hard into my eyes.

'You look at me when you talk to me,' she says. 'You got that?'

I don't answer.

She whips out a hand, cuffs my face.

'You got that?'

'OK.'

'Go on.'

'We used to meet there. After you told Becky she wasn't to see me again.'

'Cos you were a no good piece of shit.'

I drop my head. She reaches out, jerks my chin up again.

'I told you. You look at me when you're talking.'

This is hard, Bigeyes. I'm telling you. This is so hard. Looking at Ruby's like facing Becky's spirit.

'We used to meet there,' I mumble. 'And it was my fault she started coming.'

I wait for another reproach. But Ruby just fixes me with her eyes. I stumble on.

'I just couldn't cope with losing her. When she told me you said she wasn't to hang around with me again, I just . . . begged her. You know? Begged her not to stop seeing me. She was like . . . the only good thing in my life. I know I was shit. You're right. I was bad. I'm still . . . '

Her eyes go on drilling me. I force myself to keep looking at her.

'She said she'd keep seeing me but only if I tried to get better and stopped hanging about with low-life. She knew I was in big trouble. But she still kept seeing me. We had places where we met when she could get away. But this was our favourite.'

I stare down at the fish and chip shop.

Ruby's hand jerks my face back to meet her eyes.

'We used to meet there,' I say. 'She'd get the bus down. I always used to get there early. I didn't want her hanging around on her own.'

'That supposed to impress me?'

'No, I just . . . ' I shrug. 'Yeah, maybe.'

'Well, it don't.'

I feel a deep pain inside me. I don't know how much more of this I can take. Ruby leans closer.

'Go on.'

'We'd buy some fish and chips, and then come and sit in this alley, and eat and talk. She was everything in the world to me. I promise you. I'd never have—'

I see the anger flare up in Ruby's face.

'Come with me,' I say quickly.

I step out of the alley and turn down the main road. Ruby stays close. I can tell she doesn't trust me. Thinks I'm going to screw my promise and wig it without saying any more. I walk on, slow. Can't walk fast anyway. Not now.

Nothing left.

In my body or my heart.

Mother Grime goes on rippling in the night. Cars passing, smellies, taxis. Still busy, even after midnight. The Beast's more restless even than the old city. Plenty of nebs on the pavements too.

It'll be different in an hour.

And an hour after that.

Cos the Beast never sleeps. Never, ever. But two to

three in the morning's about as quiet as the Beast ever gets.

So we walk, and walk, and walk, alongside Mother Grime. Ruby hasn't spoken once since we left the alley. And neither have I. Don't really know what I've been doing, apart from walking.

Haven't been thinking.

Or watching for danger.

None of the things I usually do.

It's like I'm dead, Bigeyes. And that's cool. That's so cool.

Stop. At last.

I turn and face Ruby. She's breathing hard from the walk but the anger and hatred are still bright in her eyes.

'There better be some reason for this walking,' she mutters. Checks her watch. 'It's half past two in the morning.'

I look at her.

'That's the time Becky died. Three years ago. And this is the place.'

I turn towards the river. Bogeybum Bridge stretches away in front of us. Just a few cars and taxis rumbling over it now. Otherwise it's quiet. Almost tranquil.

I start to walk over it, Ruby beside me. And the pictures come flooding back into my head. It's going to be hard to talk about 'em. But I got to try. For Ruby's sake.

And Becky's.

'I was in big trouble.' I keep walking, slow, slow. 'And Becky knew it. I never told her any details. But she knew I was living on the edge. She was always trying to talk me out of bad stuff. She wanted me to come in to her school. There was this teacher she liked—'

'Mr Bristow.'

'Yeah, that's right. She said I ought to ask him about getting an education. Going to school and stuff. She was always going on like that.'

'Get to the point,' says Ruby.

'I was up to my neck in trouble. I'd disobeyed someone powerful and I knew he'd send people after me. I had to run, had to get out of the city, and I knew I couldn't see Becky any more. I texted her, told her I couldn't see her again cos it was dangerous for her. She texted back, said was I in the alley?'

We reach the middle of Bogeybum Bridge.

Stop.

I walk up to the rail, stare down into the black water.

'What happened?' says Ruby.

Her face is set like rock. I take a long, hard breath.

'I made a mistake. Texted back, told her yes, I was in the alley. Shouldn't have done. Told her not to come cos it was dangerous. But she did come.'

'She would have done.'

'Only I'd left the alley by then. I didn't expect her to come out.'

'I told you. She would have done. Cos she was brave.'

'I know, I know. But I didn't realize. I didn't think.'

A swirl of wind catches my face. And pictures from the past swirl with it. Mother Grime whispers below.

'I was heading this way,' I go on. 'I knew there were people hunting me and I wanted to go to ground on the south side of the river for a few hours, while I planned how to get away proper. And that's when Becky caught up with me.'

I hear an engine coming from the north side, turn and stare. Just a motorbike heading towards us. But in my head it fades and I see Becky instead. Running, running, running.

'She was running towards me,' I murmur, 'calling my name. Blade, Blade, Blade. She gave me that name. Did you know that?'

Ruby doesn't answer. I shake my head.

'Don't know how she found me this far from the alley. Must have run everywhere looking. All by herself. Didn't even think of the risk. She caught up with me here. Right here.'

I stare down at the bridge, the rail, the river below.

Motorbike chugs past, disappears. Couple of cars follow.

Silence.

Ruby mutters.

'Go on. Finish it off. Finish me off.'

'They came from the south side. They were in a van. I knew it was danger the moment I saw it.

Nobody else on the bridge. Becky didn't even notice. She was trying so hard to talk me out of running away. She wanted me to go to the police and tell 'em what I know. But all I could see was this van. I told her to run. She didn't get it. I grabbed her hand and tried to make her. Then I heard the shot.'

'No!'

Ruby claps a hand over her face. I make to reach out but she slaps me back. I blunder on.

'She went straight down. Where you're standing. I knew she was dead. No question about it. She was dead the moment she got hit.'

Ruby starts moaning.

'No, no, no.'

'I was panicking and the van was whipping in. I knew I couldn't leave Becky. I couldn't bear to. I picked her up and tried to carry her towards the north side. I was desperately hoping more cars would turn up or people or something. But it was still quiet.'

Ruby turns away, leans on the rail, crying.

I walk over, stand by her shoulder.

'It was no good. I couldn't run and carry her too. Maybe I should have stayed and let 'em kill me.'

'Maybe you should have.'

'But I didn't. I heard another shot. It missed but it was close. So I put her down.'

'Bastard.'

'I put her down.' I got tears flooding too. 'And then I ran. The van came on. I saw it over my shoulder. It stopped by Becky's body, two guys got out and heaved her over the rail into the river, then they got back in the van and came on after me.'

'Bastard.'

'But by then I was close to the north side and a couple of cars were hitting the bridge, and the guys in the van couldn't shoot cos of them, and . . . I got away.'

I fall silent.

A taxi rolls past, another, then nothing.

Just Ruby weeping, bent over the rail. And me, watching.

She turns suddenly, blares at me.

'Yeah, you got away! But not my Becky!'

I don't answer. She bustles up, slaps me hard in the face.

'You get to live and I don't even get Becky's body.

It don't never get washed up. So I got nothing. And she got nothing. Only not you. Cos you got something. You got your shit life.'

I look down. She's wrong, Bigeyes.

Cos I got nothing too. Yeah, I got my life, but what's my life worth if I got no one who cares about me? And no one I can care about? Cos I want to care. And I did care. Meeting Mary, Jaz, Becky. I did care. You know I did.

Bigeyes?

You know I did.

But Ruby hasn't finished. She slaps my face again.

'Don't you dare look down. You look up at me.'

I look up. And I know what's coming. Her eyes snarl into mine.

'And that same day,' she growls.

'I know.'

'That same day Becky goes missing, I come and find you and ask you if you've seen her and—'

'I know. I lie to your face.'

'You lie to my face. Like the worthless little bastard you are.'

'I know I was wrong.' I look down, look up. 'I couldn't face it, couldn't face you. I know I was bad. And I'm sorry. I'm really sorry.'

She gives a snort.

'And I just knew you were lying. It was written all over your face. That's why I shouted after you and said I'll kill you if you ever come back. I just wish to God I'd had the guts to carry that out when you showed up at my house.'

She turns away from me and stares towards the other side of the bridge. I watch her for a moment, clenching my fists, then walk up to the rail. She doesn't follow. I check over my shoulder. She's still facing the other way.

A car passes, another, another.

Bridge falls quiet again.

Ruby goes on standing there, crying.

I look back at the rail, reach out, start to climb. The metal feels cold and damp. It's slippery at the top and for a moment I'm scared I'll lose my grip. Freaks me bad, Bigeyes. Cos I don't want to do this the wrong way.

I want to do it right.

But I'm over now. Rail's up against my back and I got my feet snug on the ledge. I'm clasping the metal behind me and all I got to do is let go. I stare down at the black mouth.

'I hate you, Mother Grime,' I murmur. 'But I hate myself even more.'

It's all right, Bigeyes. Don't worry. This is meant to be.

I think of Mary, Jaz.

Becky.

And let go.

tim bowler

CUTTING LOOSE

In the next instalment of Blade . . .

The bridge slips from my grasp. I peer down
at the river. It's yawning in the night,
far below me, and I'm falling towards it
like a wingless bird. Dead in my body,
dead in my heart. Ready to die again.

I'm starting to breathe blood. I can feel it
pounding in my head. I got my hands moving
inside my coat and they're squeezing the knives,
just like they used to. Only it's not the same,
not now. Cos I don't love the blades any more.
I hate 'em. But it makes no difference.
My hands still find 'em.

He watches me, stretches out his arm, points the gun at my heart. I stiffen. Part of me wants to squirm backwards. Rest of me doesn't want to flinch. I keep still, somehow. No point moving anyway. Nowhere to hide in here. Close by I feel the women watching. He gives a smile, squeezes the trigger — then pulls.

Sky's lightening, see? Just a bit. But what kind of a dawn will it be? And how many times have I wondered that? I'll tell you, Bigeyes. Lots of times. That's the crack of it. Dawn after dawn after bloody dawn. I'm fourteen, Bigeyes, and I've seen more dawns than I deserve to already. And every time I see one, I ask myself if it's going to be the last.

One thing I know, Bigeyes. Whatever I can do with a knife, it's not worth dog shit now. Won't save me. Not really. Not the part of me that matters anyway. The part old Mary found. And little Jaz. And Becky. Sweet, beautiful Becky. None of them ever needed a knife. So why do I?

Tim Bowler is one of the UK's most compelling and original writers for teenagers. He was born in Leigh-on-Sea in Essex and after studying Swedish at university, he worked in forestry, the timber trade, teaching and translating before becoming a full-time writer. He lives with his wife in a small village in Devon and his work-room is an old stone outhouse known to friends as 'Tim's Bolthole'.

Tim has written nine novels and won thirteen awards, including the prestigious Carnegie Medal for *River Boy*. His most recent novel is the gripping *Bloodchild* and his provocative new *BLADE* series is already being hailed as a groundbreaking work of fiction. He has been described by the *Sunday Telegraph* as 'the master of the psychological thriller' and by the *Independent* as 'one of the truly individual voices in British teenage fiction'.